MAD AS A HATTER

SONS OF WONDERLAND BOOK 1

KENDRA MORENO

Mad as a Hatter

Sons of Wonderland Book 1

Kendra Moreno

Please do not participate in piracy.

Copyright © 2018 by Kendra Moreno
All rights reserved. This book or any portion thereof
may not be reproduced or used in any manner whatsoever
without the express written permission of the publisher
except for the use of brief quotations in a book review.

This is a work of fiction. Names, characters, businesses, places, events, locales, and incidents are either the products of the author's imagination or used in a fictitious manner. Any resemblance to actual persons, living or dead, or actual events is purely coincidental.

Edited by Michelle Hoffman
Cover art by Ruxandra Tudorica with Methyss Art
Formatted by Nicole JeRee

ISBN: 9781797414300

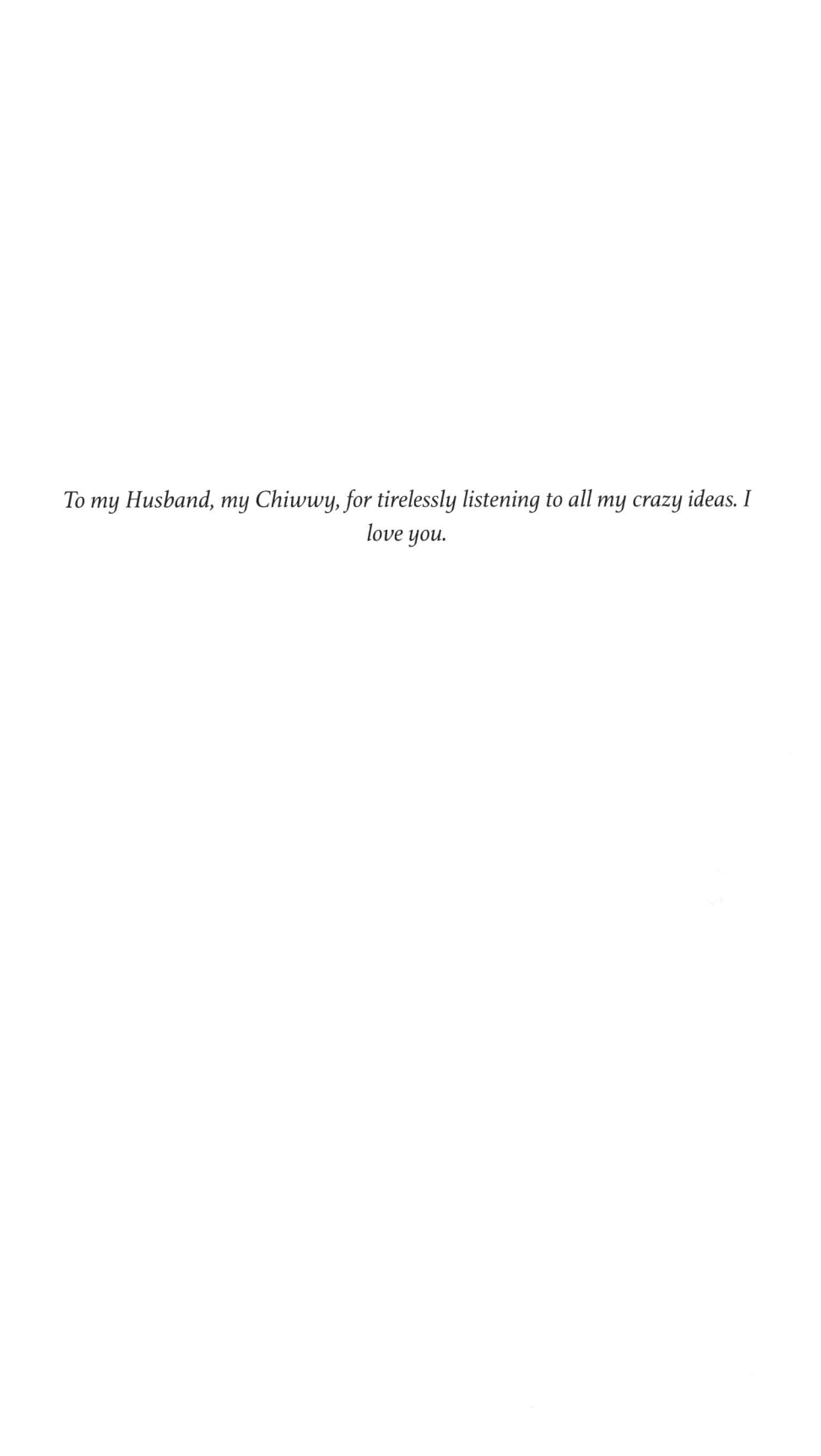

To my Husband, my Chiwwy, for tirelessly listening to all my crazy ideas. I love you.

Prologue

"You were supposed to be my friend!" Alice shouted. "You were supposed to be there for me! Where were you, Hatter? Where were you when I needed you?"

"We didn't know, Alice," the Hatter pleaded. He was manacled to the wall, blood dripping down his arms to his bare chest. His hat and his long coat had been stripped from him the moment Alice had ordered him to be thrown in the dungeons. The manacles were covered in odd symbols, the likes Hatter had never seen before. They glowed with the slightest movement and sent needles of pain into his wrists. "Time moves differently here. It isn't linear. You could have left yesterday, or tomorrow, or a year before. There's no way to track it."

"I left twenty-five years ago," she snarled. "As soon as I left Wonderland and started spewing stories of talking flowers and rabbits and Hatters, I was thrown in the asylum. My own parents paid them to take me away for fear of embarrassment. They thought I was crazy! Do you know what they do to mad people in my world?"

"Please, Alice," the Hatter tried again. "We were friends. This isn't what you want to do."

Alice grinned, stepping closer to him. She ignored his comment, continuing on as if she never heard him speak.

"Electroshock treatments. Lobotomies. Did you know they cut into my brain? Said they would fix the part that suffered from insanity. Ask me if it worked. Ask me if I screamed, and screamed, and screamed." Rage dripped from her voice, coating every word.

"You're not *my* Alice," he rasped, his voice already growing weak. Whatever was in the manacles was taking its toll.

"This is exactly who I am, who I'm meant to be. The treatments didn't work. They just made me angry. Angry at the doctor cutting

I

into me. Angry with Wonderland for showing itself to me to begin with. Angry at you for abandoning me. Now, I want to see if you can die, Hatter." She thrust her hand into his bare chest, her claws wrapping around his still beating heart. The Hatter screamed in agony, blood trickling from the corner of his lips and flowing from where her hand still lay nestled in his chest.

"Alice," the Hatter gurgled, his head slumping to his chest. "Alice." His voice was barely a whisper, the pain shutting down his body.

"No," she sneered, laughing maniacally as she ripped his heart completely from the cavity. She brought it to her lips and licked the blood, letting it drop down her chin and onto her chest. "Not Alice. Not anymore." She smiled, a deranged curl, as she crushed the heart in her hand. "I'm the Red Queen."

Chapter 1

"So, how did you come by the research, Mr. Gregory?" I ask the man shifting uncomfortably on the witness stand. He has been lying through his teeth since the moment he sat down. I knew he was lying when his eyes shifted back and forth between the defendant and the ceiling. I've been slowly leading him to dig a much bigger hole than he'd already dug himself.

"Umm." He's searching for the answer in his mind that he had been told to memorize. The poor bastard. He would lose his job after all this, something I could have helped him with if he hadn't purposely tried to cover everything up. As it stood now, he would be a casualty of the big business he works for.

"Answer the question please, Mr. Gregory," the judge prompts, watching closely. He holds a pen in one hand, jotting down notes, his glasses slid to the end of his nose. I'm pretty sure the judge knows what's up. The jury is another matter. Some of them don't care one way or the other, but the few that are invested in the case are the ones we need to win over to our side.

My clients had lost everything when the big company, Stanton Industries, had stolen their idea. All the money they had invested, down the drain. They had lost their house when they couldn't pay the mortgage. All the while, Stanton Industries was making billions from their program and not once did they credit my clients' small company, Jones Tech. Not many lawyers would have taken the case, deeming Stanton Industries too powerful to go up against. I wasn't just any lawyer, though.

"Someone brought it to my desk, one of the developers." When Mr. Gregory finally speaks, his voice cracks. Sweat beads on his brow.

"What was this developer's name?" I ask.

"I don't know. There's too many names to remember."

I flip through my notes. Each page flick makes Mr. Gregory flinch from the noise, like he's dodging bullets.

"There are six developers that could have been responsible for bringing the research to you. Six possibilities. You can't remember six names, Mr. Gregory?"

"No." He's visibly shaking now, the sweat pooling and staining the armpits of his shirt. "I'm bad with names."

"Okay. How about if I show you the pictures of the six employees? Would you be able to pick the developer out of the photographs?"

"No." He tugs at his tie before fidgeting with the buttons on his shirt. "I didn't see which one it was."

"Then how do you know it was one of the developers? Couldn't it have been Mr. Stanton, the defendant, who left this research on your desk?"

"I don't know."

"Was it not Mr. Stanton that urged you to come out with the program as quickly as possible, urging you to bypass normal procedures?"

"I don't know."

"What *do* you know, Mr. Gregory?" I ask, my voice cold. I have no respect for people who sit in silence and pretend bad things don't happen. He could have stepped up, reported the theft to someone, and he would have been protected for it. Now, he will go down with the ship.

"I only know someone dropped the research on my desk, so I handled the launch. We didn't steal any ideas. It was something our company has been working on for a while. The launch had nothing to do with the small company. I was only doing my job."

"Really?" I smirk. "You didn't know the idea was stolen?"

"No."

I turn to the judge, flipping my notebook again.

"Your honor, I'd like the bring to the jury's attention, evidence number fifty-three."

There's a visible shift in the courtroom, everyone curious about what evidence I'm bringing forward. A portable stereo is brought out, a recording device hooked up to it. The evidence had been added this morning, hardly enough time for the defense to find a way to discredit it. Voices begin to fill the room when the court worker presses play.

"They know. They know we took the idea. They're onto us. What are we gonna do?"

"Nothing. We do nothing. No one would dare take us on." The second voice matches that of the defendant, and it's low and gruff, speaking quietly.

"What if they do? They'll know we took the research and made sure to launch before they could act. Oh, God. They're gonna know. I'm gonna lose everything."

"Grow a pair, John. Say nothing, and you'll be safe. We protect our own."

The recording stops, and I meet the panicked eyes of John Gregory. The jury are mumbling amongst themselves. There's chatter in the courtroom, excitement spreading. People always love a good show, and I'm nothing if not obliging.

"Would you like to change your statement?" I ask calmly, fighting the need to curl my lips at his discomfort.

He's silent for a moment, clearly trying to figure out what to say. His eyes spin around the room wildly, seeking help. When there's nothing, he springs to his feet quickly, pointing his finger at Malcolm Stanton, the man behind the operation, and the defendant. He is the man my clients are suing. Mr. Stanton had at first offered to buy out my clients, but when they refused, knowing they had a good idea on their hands, Stanton had taken their research anyways, stealing any hope of success from them.

"He made me do it! I didn't have a choice!"

The courtroom erupts in chaos as everyone begins talking at once. The judge pounds his gavel, the THUMP, THUMP, THUMP echoing through the room, but no one is listening.

"Order!" he yells. No one stops, too hyped up at the admission.

I take the seat beside my client, a wide smile on my face as I look over at Malcolm Stanton. He had threatened me when I first agreed to take the case, telling me he'd make sure I'd never work again. But he underestimated the amount of people who have been wronged by a conglomerate. I watched my father lose his life savings when a big company stole his invention. It was an awakening for me as a child. I saw lawyer after lawyer turn him down, telling him he had no chance of winning, and that it was a pointless case. When no one agreed, it decided my career. Now, I fight for the underdogs, the ones everyone else is too afraid to represent.

My clients, a sweet husband and wife team, had worked their asses off to design the program that had been swiped from right under their noses. All because someone they trusted had blabbed about it to the wrong person. They had three children at home to feed. Stanton's company didn't care one lick about that, only seeing the program for the gem it was. So, they stole it, not expecting any repercussions for their actions. People like him make me sick.

The judge finally gets everyone to settle down before he starts winding down the courtroom.

"Do you have any further questions, Ms. Ortega?" the judge asks me. The smile is still on my face.

"No, your Honor."

"Then the jury will discuss the evidence, and you can be expected to be called back when they have reached a decision."

Everyone in the courtroom stands at the same time, filing out of the room. I smile gently at my clients to reassure them as I step out, heading for the coffee counter. I'm in serious need of caffeine since my sleep pattern is messed up from the high workloads. This case has been a difficult one, only because finding the evidence strong enough to prove malpractice has been trying. And then we had stumbled upon the tape. One of the other employees in the corporation found out the program had been stolen. She had gone through great lengths to get the evidence for us, giving us the final piece of the puzzle we needed, a direct confession of Stanton's intent and involvement. The woman had remained anonymous—for good reason—but the husband and wife team already told me she has a job as long as she wanted it with their company. Any woman with the guts to take on the Stanton corporation and the morals to know she should was a woman they wanted on their team. I'd received word the anonymous woman has already accepted.

"You're persistent. I'll give you that." The voice interrupts me while I'm taking my coffee from the barista. I throw a twenty into the tip jar, sharing my good mood.

I don't look up from adding cream and sugar for a few moments, focusing on the task. Finally, I meet the eyes of Malcolm Stanton.

"Don't you have better places to be? Like off licking your wounds somewhere?" I ask, my voice pitched between indifference and boredom.

"You haven't won yet."

I smile widely, but I don't say anything further. His eyes fill with fury as I take a sip from my coffee and walk away. Men like him hate to be ignored. They also hate being revealed as the villain. I'd have to watch my back after this case.

When we are called back into the courtroom, I take my seat beside my clients, shuffling the papers I have in front of me. There is always the possibility that the jury wants more information.

A member of the jury stands from her chair as everyone settles down, a paper in her hand.

"Please read the verdict," the judge commands. The entire courtroom holds their breath, including me. No matter how many times I do this, I still stop breathing, the tension thick enough to cut.

The woman nods and glances down at the paper.

"We, the jury, find Malcolm Stanton guilty." She stops talking as excited murmurs fill the courtroom. There are a lot of people who like to see the downfall of big corporations. The judge pounds his gavel, and everyone quiets again.

"And does the jury have suggestions?"

"Yes. We would like to recommend that eighty-five percent of the revenue from the program be paid to the plaintiffs in full. Fifteen percent is to remain among the defendant's company, for the employees who had no part in the theft."

"Your recommendations are accepted," the judge nods his head, pleased with the punishment. "Malcolm Stanton, you will be brought up on charges of fraud and theft. Future court proceedings will determine the extent of your crimes. Court adjourned." The judge pounds his gavel.

My clients jump from their seats, the wife wrapping her arms around me, tears running down her cheeks. The courtroom is a cacophony of sounds, my ears ringing from the screams of joy and surprise. Malcolm Stanton glares at me as his lawyer scrambles for purchase, trying to find something, anything to use an objection for. He will probably ask for a retrial, not uncommon for cases like these. But the verdict is solid. As the judge signs it into effect, the cheers triple in volume.

I turn as I'm pulled into yet another hug, my eyes looking out at the people leaving the courtroom. There's a man sitting in the benches, the only one not moving, his eyes fixed on me. He has blond curly hair down to his chin, the color so light, it's almost white. He's wearing a suit that seems out of place, like it's from a different era. He glances down at a watch before locking eyes with me.

This time, I stare hard. On his head, clear as day, stand two white rabbit ears. They move, one flopping down in the cute way bunnies do. I blink in disbelief. What is a guy wearing bunny ears doing in a courtroom?

When I open my eyes again, the man is gone, no sign that he had even been there. I put it out of my mind when the judge calls me forward for my signature.

Mad as a Hatter

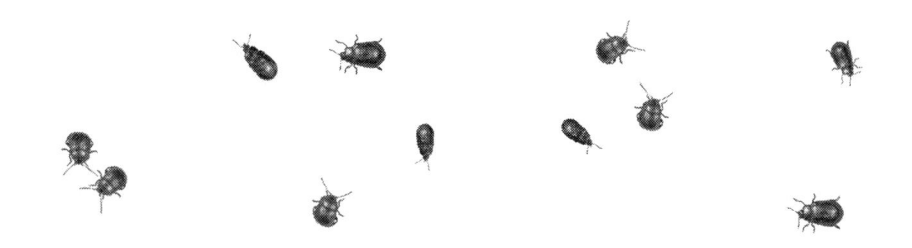

Chapter 2

I'm running, fast, through a phosphorescent forest. The colors are bright, pulsing to a beat I can't hear, leading me to somewhere I have never been. Mushrooms break through here and there, giant beasts that tower over me and seem to be reaching, reaching for something. Maybe they're reaching for me, great gaping mouths opening in their stalks. Something splashes against my face, and I wipe it away. I expected water, the beginnings of rain. Instead, my hand comes away smeared with red. I look up and wish I hadn't. Bodies, swinging, dripping, dozens. I have no idea where I am, what I'm running from, but I keep going. I ignore the wetness that begins to coat my skin. I don't want to know.

Laughter rings through the trees, reaching me as I stumble over roots that seem to rise up as I jump over them. Keep running, I chant to myself. The laughter comes again, closer. This time, it's hard to miss the menace in that laugh, the danger. This is a game, nothing more. I'm the mouse, but who is the cat?

I break through the tree line, stumbling at the suddenness of branches no longer ripping into my clothes. I look down at the fancy dress I've never worn before, the purple bright and flowing. It's ripped where the trees snagged on the material, the skirt practically in shreds. In front of me, the man from the courtroom, the one with the rabbit ears, stands, his face solemn. He raises his arm and taps his wrist watch. The simple tink, tink, tink rings through the clearing, echoing and making me flinch each time it reaches my ears. Fear skitters across his face when the laughter comes again, its source right behind me. I turn.

I shoot upright in my bed, gasping for air, the fear still sending goosebumps along my arms. My body is clammy, my hair wet from sweat. I push it away from my face, working to get my heart rate down. What an odd dream to have, I think, taking deep breaths.

Thanks to the bizarre workings of my mind, my day starts with the feeling that something is off. Things are out of step, like everything in my life just shifted a centimeter to the right. Not noticeable but enough to drive me bonkers. It takes longer to get ready, my normally tamable hair refusing to straighten, so I have to leave it wavy. My heel snaps after barely putting the stiletto on; my favorite pair. I almost leave my apartment without my briefcase, then have to turn around again because I really do forget my phone. At the boutique, overpriced coffee shop around the corner, I order a Venti instead of my usual Tall. Today is an extra caffeine kind of day.

I walk into the utilitarian law office, coffee in hand, and my employees erupt in cheers. Someone whistles. A genuine smile crosses my face. My employees are everything to me. I'm just the face and the experience, nothing more. My employees are the backbone.

I'm barely thirty-four, practically a baby in the law world, but that didn't stop me from making a name for myself. I have a reputation already, that I fight for those no one else will fight for, and I'm damn proud of it. I know my dad would have been proud to see me now. I wish he could have lived long enough. Before I had graduated with my law degree, a stroke claimed his life. It was a hard final semester, one I thought I wasn't going to make it through.

I pass the group of employees, shaking their hands and thanking them. I make a mental note to meet with finance as I make small talk and accept the congratulations. These people deserve bonuses for all their hard work. I used to be in their shoes, working for a lawyer, racking up the hours I needed to get where I am now. I had worked for a man still very important in the law world. In fact, I went up against him often since he always seems to represent the big corporations. He is a complete asshole. When I had worked for him, he thought it had given him the power to grab my ass whenever he wanted. The day I walked from that law firm with my final check was one of the most empowering moments of my life. I had flipped him off on the way out. I can still see the indignation on his face as I did it. The thought makes me smile widely like it usually does. I want my employees to know they are people, not livestock or slaves. They are so much more than just workers.

As I make my way to my office, my personal assistant comes up and begins listing my duties for the day. Jessica is a bit newer in the office, but she does a damn good job. I hope I can keep her around as long as possible, but she's currently five months pregnant. I'm already dreading her being on maternity leave but equal parts excited for her. It's her first child, a little girl. I can't wait to meet her.

"Oh," Jessica says as I take a seat at my desk. "You also have a new consultation at three. With an Alistair White."

I crinkle my eyebrows.

"Doesn't sound familiar. Did I already talk with him on the phone?"

"I'm not sure. He just called and said he needed to schedule a consultation. I assume he's bringing in a new case."

I nod my head, shuffling through the papers on my desk. "Thanks, Jessica."

I have a lot of paperwork to do before the numerous phone calls I'm obligated to make every day. The afternoon is full of appointments. The husband and wife clients from the case the day before want to come in and discuss some of the actions they're taking to protect themselves in the future. They're sweet people. I have a few more ongoing cases with appointments and a meeting with a precinct officer.

I bury myself in my work. My day is spent preparing forms for upcoming cases, assigning tasks to my employees, and scheduling various meetings. I'm so deep in my work that before I know it, it's three in the afternoon, and Jessica is poking her head in to announce Mr. White has arrived.

"Bring him in," I reply, moving my paperwork to the side. I always give my clients my full attention. The most I do is take notes, writing down anything I think is important.

When the man steps into the room, adjusting his suit jacket, I have to do a double take. It's the same man from the courtroom, the same man that had played a role in my odd dreams. He doesn't have rabbit ears this time, and I'm relieved to know he left them at home. I get all kinds in my office, but a furry is a new one.

"Mr. White, I don't believe we've met before." I stand from my seat and come around the desk to shake his hand. He hesitates a moment before placing his fingers gently in mine. Tingles shoot up my arm, not wholly pleasant. An ache starts in my bones, like there's some pressing matter I'm forgetting. It's quick, passing just as quickly as it comes, before he pulls away and moves to take a seat. I do the same and pick up my pen. "So, Mr. White. What brings you to my office?" I ask.

He grins, and I'm struck by the beauty of it. There's also something else, something dangerous, but I can't put my finger on why. Maybe it's his eyes, the glimmer in them hinting at something nefarious.

"Clara Ortega," he states, his voice a smooth tenor. "I'm afraid I come under dire circumstances."

"Is there already a court case opened? Has anyone been served?"

"No, things are just beginning, the gears barely beginning to creak into motion. But I fear it's now or never," he replies. "We desperately need you."

"Explain the situation to me." I write down 'FAST' on my notes. If the situation is as he says, everything needs to be planned for quickly. These kinds of cases are brutal.

"There is a Queen who has taken over," he begins. I keep my face neutral. It isn't unusual for my clients to exaggerate when it comes to those who have done them wrong. 'Queen' is definitely a new one, though. Most of the time, I get various curse words or 'Devil' or other such things. People like to weave their stories into epic tales. I find it makes them feel stronger to do so. "She's choking our people, killing them, ruining them, and taking everything for herself. We are at her mercy, and we can't fight back. So, we need you to set events in motion to take her down."

Mad as a Hatter

On my paper, I write 'embezzling, threats, harassments'. This sounds like one nasty CEO. Things will have to be handled delicately.

"She's abusing her power," I clarify, continuing to write on my paper. "Draining the company. Taking from the employees. How big is the company?"

"Massive," White replies. "A whole World's worth."

I write 'international' down before dropping the pen and threading my fingers together.

"I'm not going to lie to you, Mr. White. These kinds of cases are difficult, especially without proof. We're gonna have to move quickly before rumors spread. Word travels fast in the business world."

"I understand." He nods his head.

"First things first, we need proof. Any documents that show embezzlement, harassment, abuse, anything of that nature. If there's anyone in the HR department willing to get documents, that's a sure way to go." I pick up the pen again and jot down the things I'm saying, keeping track. I always like to remember what I tell my clients.

"I can get you the proof," he says.

"Perfect. We don't take any money until the case is won. If you don't win, all court fees will be paid in full by us. We only take fifteen percent of your allotment. Most of that goes towards my employees and the court."

I look up into his eyes from my notes, and my eyes widen. I blink hard, and they're still there. The rabbit ears are clear as day on his head. I look around for a moment, expecting someone to be playing a prank on me. Maybe my employees are playing a joke in celebration. I wait for someone to pop out and say, "got you!" No one does. I look at him again. There's a small smirk curling his lips.

"Is there something wrong?" he asks.

"Uh, no. Nothing at all. When can you have the documents to me, Mr. White? I'd like to begin preparing my team for this case as soon as possible." I'm watching him closely, trying to ignore the ears that are moving and twitching on his head, something I've never seen fake ears do. My eyes keep wandering to them.

"I'll take care of everything," he says, glancing at the watch on his wrist. I get a quick look at it; the thing is intricate, moving gears apparent through the watch face before he hides it away beneath his sleeve again. "Now, I really must be going. I'm late for an important matter."

"Wait, I'll need your contact information." He stands up as I ask. I copy him, rising to my feet and walking to the door of my office with him beside me.

He pulls a card from his jacket and hands it to me. Again, I'm struck by the outdated suit. He's wearing a waistcoat and ascot for crying out loud. He must be into the whole vintage revival thing. I see Hipsters, all the time, wearing things like he is. Maybe he carries around a typewriter in his free time, too, refusing to use a computer.

I glance down at the card in my hand, flipping it backwards and forward. There's nothing on the front besides a silver silhouette of a rabbit.

"This doesn't have-," I begin but when I look up, Mr. White is gone. I look around the office, searching for those rabbit ears on his head, but it's like he completely vanished, just like he did in the courtroom. The elevator dings, and the doors open, but there's no one inside or waiting. I watch, weirded out, as the doors close, and the numbers begin counting down to one.

"Jessica," I call from my doorway. She looks up at me from her desk where she'd been sorting papers. "When you get a chance, can you bring me another coffee please?"

Apparently, I'm going to need it.

I look at the clock on my desk and sigh. Another long night. It's close to midnight when I pack up my paperwork and latch my briefcase. The rest of my employees left hours ago, checking in with me before doing so. I had stayed to finish up the court papers from our last case. I look over at the giant fruit and chocolate basket sitting on the floor and smile. The husband and wife team showed up today, ecstatic and in good spirits—as they should be. I'd never be able to eat so much fruit. I plan on taking it to the office kitchen area and letting everyone have at it. I had already taken some of the chocolate, though. Can't let that go to waste.

I stretch as I stand from my chair, my joints popping from sitting in the same position for so long. I really need to look into getting one of those fancy chairs that support your spine better. God knows I spend enough time in it.

I turn off the lights in the office as I go, dropping the large space into almost darkness. The flood lights stay on, shining direct beams of light into the gloom. It gives the room a creepy feeling, like I'm being beckoned into the darkness. I shake my head to clear the thought and step into the elevator.

In the lobby, Gerald, the night guard waves to me as my shoes clack against the marble. The sound echoes, adding to the ominous vibe that seems to be following me.

"You need me to walk you to your car, Ms. Ortega?" he asks, his eyes watching the street suspiciously.

"No thank you, Gerald. I'll be fine. See you tomorrow," I reply, leaving the building and hanging a left. The employees park in the garage, but the building gave each company a designated parking spot around the side of the building. It's where I park my Jaguar. Of course, it isn't always so dark when I park there. I make another mental note to tell the building manager that lights need to be put in around the parking area. Right now, there is no lighting whatsoever. If I was any other woman, I would be worried, but I take some self-defense classes every now and then. The only way a person could catch me by surprise is if they shoot first. Apparently, the chances of that are pretty low for a woman. We get all the extra worries besides being robbed.

I pull my keys from my briefcase, their jingle loud in the silence, and I curse the fact I didn't take them out while inside. Number one rule of self-defense: don't stand there digging through your purse. Don't be distracted. I look up when there's a sound across the street, drawing my attention. At first, I don't see anything, but a flash of white catches my eyes. I narrow my gaze, trying to get a better look at a shape I can barely see when my sight seems to sharpen. Mr. White is across the street, standing without a care in the world even though everything around him is dark and seedy. Remembering I need his phone number, I wave my arm to get his attention.

"Mr. white," I call, my voice echoing.

He turns to look at me before beginning to walk away, his pace slow and lazy. Those rabbit ears twitch at a quicker rate. If it was a prank, he would have taken the things off by now. I have to assume it's some weird quirk that he has.

"Wait," I yell, stepping off the curb and running after him. Maybe he didn't recognize me. I cross the abandoned street, striding after him, the clack of my heels full of purpose. I'm maybe ten yards behind him when he turns down a dark alley. I pause at the mouth, hesitating. Everything in me screams not to go after him, not to go after a man I hardly know into a dark alley, especially one as weird as Alistair White.

"Mr. White." Even I can hear the strain in my voice, the nervous thread. "I really need your phone number, so we can begin working on your case. I'd appreciate it if you would come out of the alley."

Something stirs in the dark, and I force myself to hold my ground as Mr. White appears in the darkness, his white ears like a beacon. Forget this, I think, preparing to turn and leave.

"Ms. Ortega," he drawls, his voice taking on a sinister tone I haven't heard before.

He isn't dressed in his full suit anymore, only wearing the green waistcoat with no shirt underneath. His arms are muscled, toned, and I jerk my eyes away when I realize I'm staring. Instead of meeting his eyes though, mine land on the ears still very much on his head.

"We have to get rid of the Queen," Mr. White says, taking a step forward.

"Right." I take a half step back warily. "Your card doesn't have a phone number. I need it if we're going to be working together."

"So, you agree she needs to be taken care of?" he asks, tilting his head to the side.

"Of course. But like I said, we need to work fast."

Seemingly coming to a decision, Mr. White holds out his hand for the card, and I breathe a sigh of relief. The hairs on the back of my neck stand on end as our hands come close. I expect him to pull a pen from somewhere, and I'm prepared to offer one if he needs. I always have pens in my briefcase. What I don't expect is for him to breath on the silver rabbit silhouette and throw the card on the ground. I'm ready to ask him what the hell he's doing, but before I can, a bright light flashes on the concrete in front of me. The ground opens up, a spinning vortex of colors that picks up trash and debris in the alley and shoots it into the air. My hair flies around my face, catching against my lipstick. A whistling noise fills the passage, the kind they tell you warns of a tornado. I'm so thrown, I hardly react. I don't even back away at first, curious about what is going on.

"What the hell?" I mumble, coming to my senses and trying to back away from the thing that very much resembles the portals I see on sci-fi shows on late night TV. I fall backwards, my heels catching on the pavement, and I go down hard. It doesn't stop me from trying to scramble away, but it's no use. The whistling gets louder, and I feel the vortex pull at me, like I'm being sucked inside its gravity. I shriek as I'm yanked backwards and into the portal. My fingers latch onto the edge just before I go in completely, the asphalt digging into my palms, and I know my hands will have slices all over them. I try to pull myself out, using all the strength I have, but it does no good. White just stares at me as my fingers slip from the edge, and then I'm falling down, down, down. I scream, my stomach flipping somersaults at the sensation.

I watch as Mr. White jumps in behind me, a grin on his face, enjoying this way too much.

"Let's go kill the Queen!" he whoops.

The portal closes behind him. There's nothing but darkness.

KENDRA MORENO

Chapter 3

I blink open my eyes slowly and then immediately slam them shut again when the light shoots pain through my skull.

"What the literal hell?" I mumble, rubbing my forehead.

The piercing ache fades away, and I'm finally able to open my eyes. I wish I hadn't. I have no idea where I am, but it certainly isn't anywhere I've been before. Panic spears through me, but I squash it down. Now isn't the time to lose my head.

I take stock of my surroundings. I'm lying on a cold tile floor, like I had been dumped here and forgotten. My body aches, and I run through wiggling my toes and fingers, shifting around. Finding nothing broken or in serious pain, I sit up, relieved to see my dress and shoes are still on. Nothing like being in an unknown situation without clothes. I curse the fact that I left my jacket hanging on my chair in the office. It would have come in handy against the chill seeping into my bones from the tile.

I look at the room I'm in, having to squint my eyes to really focus. The entire room is done up in black and white diamonds, from floor to ceiling, but it's distorted, like someone dipped their finger in and swirled it around. I look away when the headache starts up again under the strain of focusing too hard. The room is trippy.

From what I can tell, the area is square, though assigning a shape to it feels wrong. It seems to switch between shapes, depending on the angle you look at it. Along the walls, are various doors, different sizes and colors. Slowly standing up, I brush myself off and go to the door closest to me, a normal-sized teal one. I grab the knob and twist, annoyed to find it locked. I move to the next one, this one so giant I have to stand on my tiptoes to reach the handle and try again. Same thing. Frustrated, I circle the entire room and try each and every knob, including the one so small I doubt my hand can even fit through. I growl in anger when the last one is the same. I'm locked in a room with no way out. My headache comes back full force.

I whirl, preparing to scream in fury, when I notice a small table in the center of the room. It sits completely alone, and I wonder how I missed it before. Momentarily forgetting the doors, I cross the room, my heels clack, clack, clacking across the tile. On the table, there is a teacup on a saucer, a purple liquid inside, with the words "Drink Me" on a plaque. Next to it is a piece of candy labeled "Eat Me".

"You've got to be kidding me," I say out loud, looking around the room again. I've obviously been kidnapped by some sick people. That or I was bashed over the head, and I'm currently lost in some sort of twisted dream. "Hello?" I call, searching the room for cameras. I don't see any, but that doesn't mean they aren't there. If I was kidnapped, these kinds of people get off on recording the action. No one answers me, so maybe I'm just dreaming. I refuse to think I might just be dead and in some sort of limbo.

I turn my attention back to the table and see a small key, one that almost blends in with the table cloth. It's then that I really take note of the material. I lean closer to inspect it. The smell hits me first, a rancid, rotting aroma that makes my nose hairs curl and my stomach roil. I reach out and touch the cloth lightly with my finger tip. The material is smooth, a kind of silicone sponginess. I jerk away in horror, realizing the only thing it could be.

"What the fuck?"

I run to one of the doors again and begin yanking on it as hard as I can. It's futile—it doesn't even so much as budge—but I'm growing desperate. I'm pulling so hard, my shoulders pop with each tug, threatening to snap out of socket.

"Let me out!" I shout. "Let me the fuck out of here!"

Realizing it's pointless, I turn and put my back against the door, breathing hard. I'm not stupid. The similarities between what is happening and the Alice in Wonderland book my mom got for me when I was young are uncanny. Someone is playing games, and I'm not sure I'm ready to face whoever could make a tablecloth out of human skin. I assume it's human skin. The texture is correct, the stitching on it showing where pieces had to be joined to form linen. Either way, it's rotting, and I have no idea how I didn't notice the smell before. Now, it fills the room, overpowering my senses.

I wrack my brain for details I remember about the book. Maybe this is a puzzle of some sort. If I win, I'll live. Isn't that how the horror movies work? Eat me, Drink me. One made Alice grow, and one made her shrink, right? That means I have to drink whatever is in that tea cup to get anywhere.

I slowly walk towards the table, covering my nose with one hand to try and block out the worst of the smell. It doesn't really work, the rot making my eyes water the closer I get. My hands are shaking with nerves when I reach out and pluck the key from the table. Then I curl my fingers around the tea cup and lift it.

"I wouldn't do that if I were you," a voice echoes behind me.

It startles me so badly that I drop the cup, the porcelain shattering as it crashes against the table. I spin, almost tripping over my heels in the process, and meet the eyes of none other than Mr. Alastair White. I let loose a sigh of relief.

"Mr. White," I sigh, placing a hand on my chest to slow my heart rate. "They got you, too. I hate to say it, but I'm thankful I'm not here alone."

The rabbit ears still twist and flop on his head, but I have bigger problems at the moment than whatever mechanism makes the things move as if they're real. Besides, I really don't want to think too hard about the similarities between the fairytale and what I'm witnessing.

"Actually, here I just go by White," he drawls, his hands in his pockets as he studies me. He's only wearing the green waistcoat, no shirt underneath, and slacks, the exact outfit I saw him wearing in the alley. I can see rolling tattoos across his body, swirling designs that I can't make out. They seem to move and shift even as he stands still. It peaks my curiosity, but I push it away for now. It isn't the time to study tattoos.

"What do you mean by 'here'?" I ask, deciding to focus on one thing at a time. If he goes by a certain name wherever we are, that means he comes here often, which means there's a possibility he's my kidnapper.

He ignores my question, instead pointing towards the table where I dropped the tea cup.

"It's a good thing you didn't drink the tea," he says.

I look, and my eyes widen at the giant hole eaten through the tablecloth and the wood. The tea still sizzles where it spilled, completely destroying the table. It begins to lean to the side, as crooked as the rest of the room. Holy Hell, I'd almost put that stuff in my body. I shiver thinking about it. I run my hand through my hair and look at Mr. White again. White, I correct myself, because wherever we are, he has been here before.

"What was in the cup?" My voice is rough with nervous energy. I'm equal parts afraid and intrigued.

"The last time the queen came through, she switched out the cup for poison. Didn't want anyone coming in that could take her down. She didn't count on me, though." He looks at the table, sadness in his eyes. "I was almost too late." He turns back towards me. "Rule Number one: Don't drink the tea here unless you trust the person giving it to you."

"How do I know who to trust?" I ask, moving further away from the table. It gives me the creeps.

"You don't." An ominous smile spreads across his face. "Rule number two: Trust no one."

"Noted." I take his warnings seriously. I'm out of my depths here, have no idea where I am, or how long I'd been passed out. I'm going to trust the lunatic with bunny ears because he's the only thing familiar at the moment.

"Now come along." White turns towards one of the doors. "We're already much too late as it is. Nothing waits for you here."

As I follow White towards an ornate gold door, I get up the courage to ask.

"And where is 'here'?"

I'm afraid of the answer, and when he turns and looks at me, that smile still on his face, I know I'm not going to like the answer.

"Why, you're in Wonderland, of course."

Yep. I knew I wasn't going to like it.

Chapter 4

I come to a screeching halt, bracing my hand against the closest wall. Deep breaths in, deep breaths out, Clara, I chant in my mind. I've been in shitty situations before. So, I'm in some sort of drug induced coma or something. No big deal. I'll just go along with White and find a way to wake myself up. I can do that.

"Did you say Wonderland?" I ask White, because I have to be sure that's what I heard. Just in case I'm not dreaming, and I'd somehow entered another dimension, one that had entire books written about it back at home. Always have the facts. That was my motto. "As in, the Wonderland from the fictitious story book?"

"Probably not the one you know." White pulls a small case from his pocket and goes to his knees in front of the door. I realize he's picking the lock when he pulls something sharp from the case before sticking it in the keyhole. There's a bunch of clicks as he twists the metal tool.

"I have the key," I tell him, holding out the metal I swiped from the table.

He shakes his head.

"This isn't some sweet fairytale place. At least, not anymore. That key is useless, nothing more than a prop to give victims false hope."

"What happened?" I toss the key to the floor and watch him as the clicks fill the room, getting louder in increments.

"The Red Queen. She's killing Wonderland, slowly and brutally."

"I must have hit my head pretty hard," I mumble, rubbing my

eyes. "And you literally have big white bunny ears on your head right now. I've been seeing them before this, but they faded away. They aren't fading now."

"They aren't bunny ears." He sounds mildly offended about the word 'bunny'. I tuck away the information for later. "They're Rabbit ears. And it's because I'm the White Rabbit." The lock gives a final loud click before the door swings open. "My ears are a part of me. The fact that you could see them in your world was an eye opener. It's the reason I was able to figure out who you are."

"The White Rabbit? As in, I'm late, I'm late for a very important date? That rabbit?" I asked, dumbfounded. I ignore the knowing who I am bit. That just seems like too much at the moment. If this is a dream, I'll have to give my imagination credit. This is like nothing I have ever thought of before.

White chuckles, but the sound is dark, a sinister vibe rolling off him in waves. I involuntarily take a step back.

"Yeah, sure. That's me," he says, looking at the watch on his wrist again. I'm struck by the gears moving in it, remembering I thought it a luxury watch at home. Now I'm thinking it's more magic than expensive. "We'd best be going. We don't want to be in the forest when it's dark." He looks around the room again. "The Red Queen, no doubt, already knows you're in Wonderland. She would have sent her Knave the moment the tea cup was touched."

I take a step forward, my heels clicking against the tiles, and his eyes fall to my feet.

"Those are going to be a problem. We're going through a dense forest."

I shrug.

"I don't really have a choice. If you had plans on kidnapping me and carting me off to Wonderland, maybe you should have warned me to wear sensible shoes."

He raises his eyebrows at my remark.

"You're taking this remarkably well." He studies me, searching for a sign that I'm really freaking out. He won't find one. The reason I'm such a good lawyer is because my poker face is flawless. I'm far from hysterical, though. Curiosity is getting the better of me, and if this isn't a dream or some sort of drug side-effect, I want to find out everything I can.

"What else am I supposed to do?" I huff. "Curl up in the fetal position and have a good cry? That's not who I am."

A genuine smile spreads across his face, warm and the complete opposite from the ones I'd seen before. It changes his appearance, so he looks more wholesome instead of the danger that usually accompanies him.

"No. Indeed, it's not." He glances through the doorway, and I get a view of outside for the first time. There's trees, a lush forest even if it's dark. Some of the plant life is glowing, much like the dream I had this morning, but besides that, I can't really tell much else.

"I thought you said we didn't want to be in the forest at night?" It sure looks dark to me.

"We don't," he replies, meeting my eyes briefly. "That's how the forest looks during the day."

Wow, I really don't want to know what it looks like at night then. Talk about nightmares.

"Before we go out there," he continues. "We need to discuss a few more rules."

"Why?" I ask, watching as a beautiful butterfly comes through the door. I stare in wonder at its iridescent blue and pink wings fluttering around me. As it draws closer, I notice the oddness of its body. Both sides look like a stinger, no head I can see. When two eyes blink open on the wings, my heart stops, but when it lets out a high-pitched snarl that makes my skull feel like it's cracking, I damn near pass out.

White smacks the thing from the air, cutting off the sound as he squashes it beneath his boot. I hold my head as he looks at me pointedly.

"Wonderland isn't safe. Nothing is here. Don't let the bugs touch you," he lectures. "Most of them drink blood."

I take a big breath. This just keeps getting worse and worse.

"Got it," I grunt. The ache in my skull finally begins to ebb, and I drop my arm to my side.

"And don't go near the talking flowers."

"I thought the talking flowers are nice?" I ask. It's a stupid question. There aren't skull-shattering butterflies or poison tea in the original tale. Why would I think the dumb flowers would be friendly?

"They like their meat rare," is the only reply I get. I feel the blood drain from my face. Fuck that. I'm not going to become dinner for the fauna.

"Why the hell am I here?" I ask. "Why me?"

He looks at me from the doorway where he had been watching the trees. There's multiple emotions in his eyes, bouncing between sadness and anger.

"Because Wonderland needs you, Clara."

"Surely, there are others you can bring?"

He shakes his head. "You were prophesied to be here."

"I decide my own fate," I say, a frown spreading across my face. It's the words I had repeated to myself my whole life.

"Of course, you do," he mocks, grabbing my hand. "But Wonderland has other ideas." He pulls me through the doorway behind him. "Now come on. We're late."

"Where are we going?" I ask. Because why not? I want to be informed before I get eaten by something in the jungle. Or worse.

"To see the Hatter." There's no emotion in his voice as he answers, just cold indifference.

Of course, I think. The next logical step.

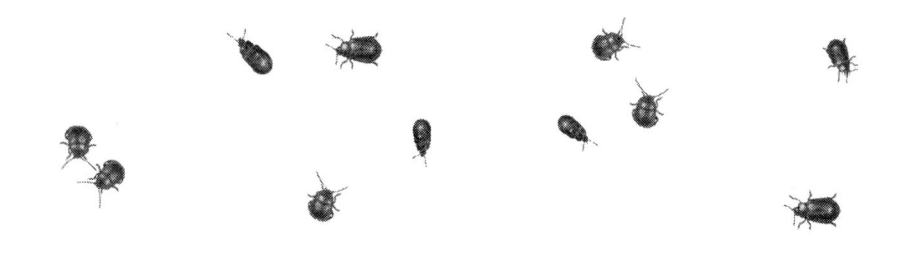

Chapter 5

Wonderland is nothing like the books. The forest is so dark, it would be pitch-black if it wasn't for the phosphorescence that emanates from the plant life. The trees glimmer, some sort of neon-colored sap dripping down their trunks, resembling blood more than anything. Giant mushrooms rival the trees, taller and wider than the redwoods I'd seen on the nature channel. Their undersides, the soft fleshy parts of them, glow in various colors, sending a warm incandescence across the forest floor. It gives everything a relaxing feel, even if it is far from relaxing. Every now and then, I'd catch a great, gaping mouth open on the stalk of a mushroom, sharp teeth curling into a smile as black eyes watch me, waiting for me to slip up and step too close. I stay right on White's coat tails.

The bugs are worse than mosquitoes, constantly buzzing around us and trying to land on me. White just smacks them away but I'm equally parts terrified of touching them as I am of one biting me. The result is a sort of flailing panic as I try to keep them away from me.

"You don't have any bug spray?" I huff at White. How he's able to not trip over the uneven ground is a mystery to me. Even if I wasn't in heels, it would be treacherous. I'm certain the roots and vines move to purposely trip me. After I see one of the trees blink at me, I decide that isn't so farfetched of an idea. The trees, apparently, like to cause trouble, and I'm the newest unsuspecting victim.

"It wouldn't work here," White replies, glancing back to check on my progress. "The bitter smell of it attracts them."

"So, use something sweet."

White's eyes widen before a look of contemplation crosses his face.

"Not a bad idea."

I put my hands on my hips and look up into the glowing canopy, taking deep breaths to get my heart rate under control. I'm sweating like crazy, the tripping taking a toll on me. Note to self: never wear heels again if there's a possibility of trekking through a dangerous forest. Just as I move to follow White, there's a sharp pinch on my forearm. I yelp, jerking away. There's a bug on my arm, this one with a face. Well, a mouth. I don't see any eyes, only a round hole lined with layers upon layers of teeth. It looks like a leech with dragonfly wings. The wings glow a brilliant pink, but its body is a slimy brown.

As I look at it in horror, blood dripping down my arm where it bit me, it growls and my instinct kicks in. I smack it from my arm, pick up the closet club-like stick I can find, and proceed to beat the ever-living hell out of it. I might let out the same battle cry I use when killing spiders that manage to find their way into my apartment. It's the same battle cry that got my neighbor to call the cops once, thinking I was being murdered. Bless the old woman's heart for trying to help. The embarrassment of explaining the spider situation to the attractive cops who showed up at my door hadn't been so fun.

I'm proud to say that once I finish beating the bug, there's nothing left but a small patch of brown and phosphorescent pink. Don't judge me.

"Did it bite you?" White asks, urgency in his voice.

"Yes. My arm." I hold it up for him to take a look.

He reaches into a leather pocket on his belt loop. I never realized he had the pockets, and I'm surprised to see quite a few of them. I'm intrigued by what he carries in them. It's a bunch of little fanny packs. I smirk at the thought as White opens a vial, pulling the cork off the top with his teeth. He spreads a green salve on the wound, the sensation cold. The itch that had accompanied the bite disappears.

He doesn't talk, and I decide not to ask, too afraid of the answer. I'm pretty sure I almost died, though.

We continue on our way, terrifying screeches and shrieks filling the air. There's a particularly intense bellow from far away, and even though I'm certain we're not close to it, I still feel it through the ground.

"What the hell is that?" I ask, my eyes wide.

"Bandersnatch." He doesn't seem worried at all even though I damn near wet myself. "You don't want to run into one of those. They're the Queen's creatures. If the bellow gets closer, cover your ears. It won't stop the pain, but it might stop your ears from bleeding."

"Fantastic." I shake my head. "There's absolutely no way this can be real. I'm dreaming. I have to be. Granted, my dreams are never this vivid."

White smirks at me. "You still don't think this is real?"

"How can it be? There's just no way," I mumble.

White studies the ground in front of him before leaning down and picking up a thin stick. He bends it back and forth before nodding his head in satisfaction. Without warning, he whips the stick across my ass, leaving behind a stinging pain. I shriek in surprise, jumping away from him.

"What the hell was that for?"

He's grinning, mischief twinkling in his eyes.

"You thought it wasn't real."

"So what? How does hitting me have anything to do with that?"

"You can't feel pain in your dreams, right?"

I stare at him, rubbing my ass as it dawns on me.

"And that just hurt." I frown at him when he nods his head.

"Logically, this has to be real."

"Logically," I parrot mockingly. "I could have just pinched myself. You didn't have to hit me."

"But where would the fun be in that?"

I shake my head at the grin on his face. He had enjoyed that way too much.

I take another step, frowning over the exchange. A particularly persistent root rises into the air, catching the heel on my stiletto, and I pitch forward so fast I have no time to catch myself. Before I can hit the ground, White's arm wraps around me from behind, stopping me inches from face planting. I stare into the eyes of a small flower, it's petals white and mocking. It smiles at me, razor sharp teeth revealed at its center. A forked tongue flicks out, tasting the air, tasting me. I gulp as White lifts me back up. He lets me gain my footing again before he lets go.

"Watch your step," he grunts, his amusement from a few seconds ago gone. "It's best to step high."

"Yep." My heart is going crazy. If I don't have a heart attack before this nightmare is over, I'll consider myself lucky. Not nightmare, I correct myself. This is all somehow real. "Was that one of the talking flowers you mentioned?"

White glances at the tiny flower, kicking at it with his boot. It snarls in rage, attempting to bite through the hard rubber. White frowns and stomps on it, grinding his toe into the ground. When he steps away, there's bright red mixed in with the white petals. I cringe and look away, disturbed by the brutality.

"That one was just a seed. The worst they can do is nip you. It's the big ones you gotta watch out for."

I glance at the bright spot on the dark forest floor one more time before I follow after White, my shoulders tense. We don't have trouble with any more bugs.

We finally break through the tree line, a clearing spread before us. In the center, there's a cute little cottage, vines growing up its walls, smoke coming from the chimney. It's exactly the kind of house I'd expect the Hatter from the book to have. Which is why I immediately feel suspicious. Nothing is this innocent in the Wonderland I'm coming to know.

"It's . . . cute," I say, staring warily at it.

"Look closer," White mutters, his ears twitching in agitation.

I do as he says, squinting hard until the sight before me begins to shimmer and change. When the true house is revealed in the clearing, I feel my stomach drop out from underneath me. That feeling you have when you're on a roller coaster and suddenly, you're free-falling? That's what I feel when I behold the monstrosity that is the Hatter's house.

At first, the cabin had been light colors, pinks and blues and pastels, happy almost. Now, it moves between black and a dark, royal purple, the colors shifting like a dark reflection in water. It's massive, resembling a castle now more than a cottage. Gargoyles stand guard on the roof, their faces twisted and sneering as I look into their eyes. When one ruffles its wings, I take a step back. The gargoyle doesn't move again, but its eyes focus on me, the intruder.

"This is the Hatter's house?" I ask. Another stupid question, but I have to ask. I'm not sure I want to meet the master of this mansion.

White nods his head, choosing not to speak. I appreciate the consideration. He knows I'm trying to digest the new information. The place seems in disrepair, desperately needing some TLC. Windows are broken here and there. Some of the stone is worn away in some places, chunks sitting at the base where they fell. There's a porch at the entryway, but it leans heavily to the side, the boards lifted up and coming unnailed. The harder I look at the house, the worse it appears. I turn my head, and I realize the whole house is crooked, like someone lifted one side the barest hint.

There's an aura around it, a dangerous air that makes my skin crawl. I feel threatened, my fight or flight instincts rearing their heads, tussling for control. From inside the house, chilling laughter filters out. I lean a bit more towards flight.

"Is this like the house from Hansel and Gretel?" I whisper. I don't know why I do. "Leading children inside, so they can be eaten?"

White laughs and shakes his head.

"The witch would be safer than the Hatter. At least with her, you know what to expect."

"Then why on Earth are we coming to see him?"

It doesn't seem smart to meet up with someone worse than a witch who ate children. Or is that an exaggeration? I'm not sure if I trust White's word. He could be teasing me for his own amusement.

"It's prophesied." He stares at the front porch.

As I watch, the door flies open, bright light spilling from the open doorway. A man steps out, a top hat sitting gracefully on his head. He throws his arms wide, a manic smile on his lips.

"Welcome home, Clara," he shouts, his voice echoing around the clearing.

His voice is tinged with barely concealed madness, making my heart skip a beat. I take a step back, my eyes wide.

Heart attack, here I come.

Chapter 6

"Cut it out, Hatter," White hisses at the man standing on the porch. "There's no need to freak her out more so."

At first, my mind can't quite comprehend anything but the mad glint in his eyes, the intense 'back away' vibes that crawl across my skin. I school my features, refusing to cower before him. For whatever reason, White thinks meeting the Hatter is important, so I'll just stand here. No one will know my heart is beating a million miles a minute. White's ears twitch towards me, and I curse under my breath. Maybe White knows my heart is trying to thump out of my chest, after all.

As I look, really look, at the Hatter, I'm able to see past the insanity and ignore the instinct to run ingrained in me. He's dangerously attractive, emphasis on dangerous. He wears a pair of black leather pants and a long purple jacket, the end brushing the back of his knees. It's an old-fashioned style and seems to be velvet, but I'm not a hundred percent sure. After the tablecloth fiasco, I'm not taking anything at face value.

He isn't wearing a shirt underneath the jacket. It gives me a nice view of his chest. I can tell he's muscular but lean, more like a slightly bulked-up runner. The signature top hat is perched on his head, frayed and worn. His maroon hair flops down over his forehead, threatening to hide one golden eye.

Those glittering eyes are rimmed in coal, and his lips are painted black. His jawline looks like it can cut glass. I'm startled to find him beautiful, a bit entranced with him. He's not anything like I expected.

There's this air about him, dangerous and threatening. White essentially said the same thing. I shouldn't underestimate the Hatter. There is more to him than I see.

As I study him, I realize the Hatter hadn't answered White. Instead, his eyes are fixed on me, seemingly appraising me the same way I have been doing to him. His gaze drops to the still seeping wound on my arm, and his entire demeanor changes. Anger clouds his face as he leaps from the porch, heading right for me. I don't move as he snatches the injured arm and inspects it closely. Something whispers to me that I'm in no danger. I don't know if I should listen to it or not.

"You let her get bitten?" he accuses, glaring at White.

His grip is like steel around my wrist, but he isn't hurting me. He's gentle, taking care not to squeeze too roughly.

"I put the antidote on it," White grumbles, annoyance in his words.

Hatter looks up into my eyes, the gold sparkling as they study me. I open my mouth, intending to say something, anything, to break the intensity, but nothing comes out. There's a slight tick of his lips, like he's fighting a smile before he turns and storms towards the house, pulling me behind him. White sighs loudly but follows us.

I don't have much time to look around the house as we barrel through the doorway, Hatter dragging me quickly behind him. He jerks me to the left into a gigantic room that looks like its intended purpose is for hosting extravagant parties. So far, I've encountered rotten smells, but this room is like a breath of fresh air, the smell of blossoms reaching my nose first. There are giant chandeliers hanging from the ceiling, the crystals smoky with dust. Vines climb along them, reclaiming them back into nature. The entire room is the same, flowering vines climbing along the walls, trees sprouting from the marble. I'm thankful none of them seem to have faces. It's as if the plant life has no idea they're inside a house, taking up space in a ballroom. It gives the entire room an enchanted feeling, like I just stepped into a fairytale. I suppose I actually did, though this one is closer to the grim versions than the modern one.

Dissecting the ballroom, spanning the entire space, is a long table set with tea pots and dishes. I swallow the giggle that threatens to come up. This is no time to get hysterical. Especially if I'm about to sit down to a tea party with the Mad Hatter like I suspect. We power past dozens of empty chairs, heading for the far end of the room. My heels clack double time on the vine-covered tiles, barely keeping me upright. I lose my footing several times only for the Hatter to tug and steady me again. If I wasn't so far outside my element, I might have been annoyed.

As we near the seat at the head of the table, I begin to notice we aren't alone. Sitting in a few of the chairs close to the end are creatures the likes I have never seen before. There is a man with antlers growing from his head, flowers blooming from them like a tree. He wears no shirt, and he looks at me as I'm dragged past, a peaceful smile on his face. Another creature appears more like a pig than a person, but she sits upright, and wears pearls more elegantly than I could ever pull off. There is one other person at the table, a woman with great curling horns. When she looks at me and smiles, I realize her eyes are slit like a goat. She opens her mouth as she waves, a bleat coming out instead of words. I take this all in remarkably well. This is Wonderland, after all, and following the encounters I have already had, this is a cakewalk. Odd people and creatures are to be expected.

I'm dead certain I'm not dreaming now. I'm not creative enough to make this stuff up.

Hatter stops at the end of the table and pulls out the first chair, gesturing for me to sit. I take the seat gratefully. As soon as I scoot in, I slip off my heels under the table. No one will know, but I'm not wearing the blistering things a moment longer. I'm pretty sure my feet are bleeding at this point. They aren't made for falling down a rabbit's inter-dimensional portal and trekking through a forest.

The Hatter takes the head chair. As he sits down, he throws his jacket tails behind him with more flair than I could manage on a good day. He looks out over the table.

White trails in behind us, clearly exasperated. He watches as the Hatter lifts lids on the teapots and checks their contents.

"I told you," he says, rolling his eyes. "I gave her the antidote."

The Hatter chooses a black teapot with a picture of a skull on the side and begins pouring the liquid into a delicate mint green teacup.

"The antidote for what?" I ask, finding my voice. It's the first time I've spoken in front of the Hatter, and he tenses.

He looks up at me, his hands still pouring the tea, like it's second nature by now. I suppose it should be. He must have poured thousands of teapots.

"You were bitten by a Beezle," he informs me, his honey voice sliding along my bones and waking me up in a way I hadn't been in a long time. "They inject a poison when they bite. For all intents and purposes, you should be dead." A manic gleam enters his eyes, his head tilting to the side. "Or perhaps, you're already dead. You're sitting at my table, after all."

"She's alive," White interjects, purposely staying back away from the table. I look at him in worry, wondering if I'm doing something I'm not supposed to. Had there been a rule about not sitting at the Hatter's table?

"Would serve me right," the Hatter mutters. "Would serve me right, yes it would."

"Hatter," a voice calls from the doorway. "We have another arrival."

I study the man speaking from the doorway, realizing with amusement that he has mouse ears on his head and a tail peeking from behind him. The ears look pretty rough, chunks missing from both and a piercing here and there randomly. They don't seem to follow the pattern most piercings do, sparkling everywhere besides the rim of his ear. He's dressed in a fancy suit, though it's dirty and ill-kept. Must be the Dormouse, I think. The Dormouse is always with the Hatter in the books.

Then my attention shifts to the man that strides in after the Dormouse. There's a rattle, and I look at Hatter just in time to see his face fall, sadness creeping across his expression. I have the sudden urge to take his hand. I have to physically curl my fingers into the material at my lap to stop the urge.

The newcomer walks down the table and takes a seat directly across from me. He's beautiful and golden, though older by far than any Wonderland inhabitant I have seen so far. His hair is a brilliant blond with streaks of grey just starting to take over. His face is kind as he looks at the Hatter, a smile on his lips. I get a sense of peace from him, the same as I had gotten from the other guests. There is a crown atop his head, a simple gold band, pretty but masculine.

"Welcome to the tea party, your majesty," The Hatter says sadly.

The man nods and lifts a teacup, taking a sip before sighing deeply.

"It's been so long since I've had good tea," he groans, his eyes closing in pleasure. I get this sudden feeling of hopelessness from the man—king?—as he savors the drink. It passes quickly, more like a residual speck of his prior feelings.

Hatter turns his eyes back on me, and the emotions switch instantly from sadness to delight.

"Won't you have some tea, Clara Bee?"

"Uh, White told me not to take tea from anyone," I reply hesitantly, my eyes jumping from White to Hatter.

The Hatter suddenly slams his fist on the table, making the dishes rattle. The other guests don't react, drinking their tea lazily, but I damn near jump out of my chair, my heart skipping a beat in my chest. My eyes are wide as I lean away from the Hatter. My hands clench the sides of the chair hard.

"I said drink the tea!" Hatter shouts, angry. His face softens when he sees how tense I am. "Please," he adds, cringing.

He holds the cup out to me. I look at White again. I don't exactly trust him—he had tricked me, after all–but he seems to want me alive. He nods his head in encouragement, unaffected by the Hatter's outburst.

"Hatter won't hurt you," he says, his ears twitching. I'm not sure if that's a sign of agitation or nervousness.

I turn my gaze back on the Hatter, still holding the teacup out towards me, his hands barely shaking. He's slightly smiling, the corner of his lip twitching.

"Please," he says again, and I find myself reaching forward to take the cup from him. I realize my own hand is shaking when a bit of the tea splashes onto the table.

"So, I can trust you?" I ask, hesitantly.

His eyes sparkle as the smile spreads across his face.

"No," he says. "Trust no one in Wonderland. Not even yourself."

Chapter 7

I take the tea cup with trembling fingers, making sure not to spill any more as I set it in front of me. Remembering the last cup of tea I almost drank, I pick up a spoon and swirl it in the lavender liquid. Nothing. No steam or answering sizzle. I set the spoon back down on the table and pick up the cup again.

"Good." The Hatter nods. "You're learning already." He tilts his head to the side. "A smart Clara Bee, you are," he sings.

I lift the cup to my lips and take a hesitant sip. I close my eyes as the flavor hits my tongue. I'm pretty sure I moan as the taste of ambrosia floods my mouth. My whole body warms. I have no idea what it is I'm drinking, but it certainly can't be tea. I've never had anything like it. Tilting my head back, I down the entire teacup before placing it back on the saucer it came from. My head feels a bit fuzzy, the tips of my fingers tingling.

I open my eyes slowly, feeling like I'm coming down from a high; my vision is even blurry. I'd had the same feeling once when I tried some sort of pill in my college days. Ironically enough, my friend had said it was called Wonderland. What are the odds? When my vision clears, I stifle a squeak when the Hatter's face comes into view. He must have moved when I was drinking the tea. Either he's a ninja, or I was so absorbed with the tea, I didn't hear him move. Now, he crouches beside me, his face level with mine, as he looks at me with wonder in his eyes. There's something else there, too. A heat I can

43

feel, the same heat answering in my own body. I shift uncomfortably, staring into the Hatter's golden eyes.

"It's been so long since I've had tea with the living," he whispers. "I forgot, I forgot."

Hatter leans forward, his hand coming up towards my face. It's the first time I notice his nails are painted black. Normally, the detail wouldn't do anything for me besides thinking the man is high maintenance. On him though, it fits his personality, and I find I like it. His fingers touch the corner of my lips, tickling with the slight touch. When he pulls his hand away, there's a bead of moisture on the tip of his finger, a bit of tea that had clung. As I watch him, he sticks the finger in his mouth and sucks it off, his eyes locked with mine. He pops it free and smiles.

"If it was up to me, Ms. Clara Bee would sit forever and sip my tea," he sings softly. "Ms. Clara Bee."

I watch him, weirdly enthralled. There is something calling to me, begging to be acknowledged. I find myself leaning slightly towards him, like he's pulling me into his gravity. It's a pleasant feeling, like I'm meant to be there.

"What was in the tea?" My voice is husky, and I cough to try and cover up the fact it's because of the Hatter.

He smiles wickedly.

"Poison."

I feel the blood drain from my face. Had I been tricked? Was this all some ruse to get me here and kill me?

"What?"

"The anti-venom for the Beezle," he says. "It's made with its poison." He looks at me thoughtfully. "Clara Bee will live to see another day to spend with me." Singing, again. I'm beginning to see a pattern.

"So, you saved me?" I ask softly, a small smile curling my lips when I realize I had been worried for no reason. He was only trying to save me. I'm already softening towards the lunatic. Whatever that said about me, I don't want to know. I'm enjoying the intrigue I feel either way.

"Yes," he replies, that grin still on his face. He leans closer, entering my space, but I don't pull away. I don't even think to. "Nothing is free in Wonderland. I'd like a kiss for payment."

I wrinkle my nose in confusion.

"A kiss? Seriously? Right now?"

Even I can tell my voice is breathy, and I curse the telltale sign in my head. His face softens when he hears the tone.

"Not now. Not now." He leans away from me and claps his hands together, making me jump again. He stands. This close, I notice the muscle rippling across his stomach, the chiseled abs that were easier to ignore when I was wary of him. Now, they're right in front of my face, and the ache to touch slams into me hard, but I do my best to ignore it. Trouble. The Hatter is trouble.

"Gentle Creatures," he calls to the four other guests at the table. "It's time."

They all set their teacups back on the saucers and stand, happiness apparent on all their faces. That sense of peace increases, and I find myself wanting to go with them, to find the same calm as they have.

"Come along, old friend," the Hatter says to the latecomer, squeezing his shoulder affectionately.

"Would you tell my wife I love her?" the man asks in a daze, the crown on his head catching the light and sending sparkles around the room. It makes me blink when they shine across my eyes.

The Hatter hesitates. I can see it. His eyes look away from the man and find me instead. Whatever he sees seems to steady him, and the next time he speaks, he sounds saner than I've yet to hear from him. He smiles before returning his attention back to the man.

"When she joins you, you can tell her we all did." His voice is warm when he says it, echoing of long ago memories. I don't ask, but I file it away for later.

And then the Hatter is leading them off, further into the ballroom and towards a particularly overgrown section in the back. Giant Mushrooms arch over something, but I can't see where exactly they go. I assume there's some sort of door there. The mushrooms don't move; no mouths open as the people walk towards them. They leave White and I behind in silence.

"Where are they going?" I ask White as I lean to the side to try and get a better look. There's a bright flash, but that's all I can make out. The growth is too thick, forming a wall between us and them.

"The Hatter's tea party is the last stop before the Hereafter," White answers, sadness on his face. "Hatter sits with them all."

"Those people were dead?" Surprise catches me off guard. I had been sitting with dead people, and I hadn't even known it. "They didn't look dead."

"They look more alive than when they were living." He meets my stare. "We shed our misery when we die. And the Hatter," he pauses, his eyes haunted. "The Hatter sees us in both skins."

Chapter 8

White leads me through corridors and twisted hallways, confusing me with each turn until I'm so hopelessly lost, I can't think straight. Everything is weird, like I'm having a bad LSD trip. I expect nothing less from Wonderland, though. I keep expecting to run into more creatures in the hallways—the house is huge, after all —but save for Dormouse and the Hatter, I see no one else. It makes the giant house feel abandoned, more like a Colosseum than a home. There's no warmth in the walls, a chill permeating the air.

I lose track of our direction early on, coming to terms with the fact I can't escape if I want to. Not that I want to. My curiosity has been peaked, and I find myself more and more drawn to the Hatter. It's one of my weaknesses, that curiosity. If my mom was still alive, she'd be rolling her eyes at me right about now. She always used to say I was attracted to the odd ones. I guess she was right.

Finally, we come to the end of a corridor, and White stops before a dark-purple door. There is a silhouette painted on the wood, right in the center. It's of a teapot pouring into a teacup. It seems appropriate for the Hatter's house, but I wonder why the other doors don't have the same detail. White pushes open the entry, a loud creak breaking the silence, and I follow him inside.

The room . . . isn't what I was expecting. Not that I'm expecting a four-star hotel or anything. I knew the house didn't seem taken care of. I knew it was worn and leaning, but I assumed the room would at least be clean.

The entire area is covered in a layer of dust so thick that I immediately feel my nose tickle, a sneeze right on the verge of escaping. It's like no one has entered the room in decades, like it was sealed shut. I almost feel like I'm in uncharted territory when I realize my shoes leave prints in the dust.

White doesn't seem bothered by the dust as he walks inside a few steps and gestures for me to follow. I try not focus too hard on the little clouds that rise with each of his steps. His nose twitches, so slightly that I barely catch it.

"When the Hatter is finished, he'll come by and get rid of the dust." White's voice is completely void of emotion, like he's absolutely bored with the turn of events.

I step into the room a few more paces, looking around me, putting White at my back.

"Why am I here?" He doesn't answer. I turn to ask him again only to find he's left. Figures.

Looking at the room, I realize it's like someone flipped the entire thing on its head. There's furniture hanging from the ceiling, a chair, a table, a lamp. The lamp is even turned on, giving off a hazy beam of light through the dust. There's a chandelier standing straight up in the center of the room, growing right from the floor. My lips quirk at the oddness. The bed seems like it might have been an afterthought, a giant four poster monstrosity with a canopy. It's as dusty as everything else, and although I can tell the bedding is purple, I can't tell what shade. The closer I look at the bed, though, I realize there's something off about it, too, but I can't place my finger on what. Maybe the posts are shaped weird?

I move towards a doorway in the room, propped open. It leads into a bathroom more luxurious than I had at home, or, it will be, once it's clean. There's a clawfoot bathtub in the center of the room, big enough for two. I ignore the images that pop into my head with that thought, and I move further inside.

The faucets are molded, grotesque creatures in silver. They have frighteningly sharp teeth where the water flows from. The sink faucets follow the same idea, although I can see there are different creatures sculpted for each one. They're almost beautiful in a scary sort of way.

"Clara Bee," a voice dripping with sex and violence calls from the bedroom. It isn't the Hatter. It certainly isn't White.

I whirl around, dust spinning with me, creating a rising cloud as I look back through the doorway and into the room. My heels slide in the thick grime coating the floor, but I keep them steady. I don't see anyone in the room, but I know I didn't imagine it. On the bed, I can see a spot where the dust has been disturbed, the imprint of a body, but there's no one there. Someone had been lying on the bed.

"Hello?" I call warily as I step closer. My hand wraps around a heavy candelabra that is on a table right outside the doorway. It's shaped like some sort of monster worm, razor sharp teeth opening for a candle to be placed in. I don't look too closely at the details. It's golden though, and heavy.

"What do you plan on doing with that?" the voice asks.

Confused, I stare harder at the imprint when I see no other signs of disturbance. Slowly, a grin begins to form over the bed, exactly where the dust is moved. I'm pretty sure my eyes pop out of my head when two eyes blink at me from the darkness.

"Cheshire," I whisper, because who else can it be? I keep the candelabra raised like a weapon. Trust no one.

A man slowly comes into focus, those eerie yellow eyes watching me. He has a punk rock vibe going on, and at home, I'd think he was in a metal band. He has shaggy dark-grey hair, streaked with blue that falls over his forehead in that messy look some guys just pull off. It looks like he might style it back a lot, but right now, it's more like he's been running his hands through it. There are big cat ears on top of his head. One ear has piercings running up the edge of it. Both are missing small nicks here and there, and scars glow bright-pink. He's lounging on the bed like he owns it, a grey and blue tail draping over his hip, twitching lazily.

"You know who I am," he says, grinning wide and sinister. I immediately realize I need to be on guard around him.

"Only from the stories at home," I reply, eying the leather jacket and motorcycle boots he's wearing. "Though none of them describe you the way you look now."

"How do they describe me?" he asks lazily, but I can tell he's coiled strength and danger. I know he can be off the bed quicker than I can react, tearing my throat out if he wants.

"You're just a cat with a wide smile." I clench the candelabra tighter. "And you're one of the good guys, I think."

Cheshire's eyes begin to twinkle as he sits up on the dust-covered bed. He crawls across the comforter, stalking me like a panther, dust billowing around him in clouds. It does nothing to detract from his attractiveness. As he moves, his body shifts, his clothing fading away to reveal fur sprouting from his skin. His canines sharpen, peeking from the corner of his lips. He looks more like the cat he is now. He's still humanoid—there's no mistaking he's a man—but he's covered in the grey fur, blue stripes giving little touches of color.

"Like this?" he asks, grinning like a shark.

"No." My voice sounds strangled when I answer. "Definitely not like that."

Cheshire has a magnetism the same way the Hatter does. While I can appreciate how sexy he is, I don't feel the same pull as I do to the Hatter. Something in me calls for him and not this teasing, dangerous man in front of me. Something tells me that Cheshire is all rebel, bad boy. Not my style. Nope, apparently, I like the crazy ones.

Cheshire laughs at my discomfort and transforms back into the leather-wearing man faster than I can follow. He stands from the bed and shakes the dust off, beating his jacket to remove the grime. That sneeze threatens to overtake me again as I watch him closely. He never acknowledges my earlier comment.

"Are you on the good side here?" I ask, my body tense. I don't know what I'll do if he says he's on the bad side. Maybe I'll bash him over the head with the candelabra and take my chances with the maze of hallways outside.

He looks at me, curiosity in his eyes. Guess that makes two of us.

"I'm on nobody's side but my own, Miss Clara Bee," he says.

"Why does everyone keep calling me that?" I growl, frustrated with feeling outside the loop. I need more information in a place meant to confuse me. I need to get my head straight.

"Because you are prophesied," he replies, shrugging like it's completely normal to have a prophecy written about you. Perhaps, it is common in Wonderland.

"Prophesied to do what?"

There it is, the question that has been bugging me since I was dragged through a rabbit portal into Wonderland, the question no one seems to want to answer. But I need to know, my very soul calls for an explanation.

Cheshire is suddenly in front of me, stopped barely a foot away. My breathes stutters as I look up into his face, my eyes wide. The candelabra is sandwiched between us, useless at this point. Stupid Clara, stupid, I think. You should have been paying better attention.

"You're the first to bring about the fall of the Red Queen, Clara Bee. The first of the triad. The first to bring a Son of Wonderland to his knees."

My jaw drops, and I stop breathing. Cheshire winks at me, completely nonchalant.

"What?" I choke.

Chapter 9

The door slams open and bangs against the wall hard enough that I think there might be a hole in the wall from the knob, but I don't look away from Cheshire. I know I'm not supposed to turn my back on a predator or give him the opportunity to strike. The grin on his face is dripping malice, whether for me or something else, I don't know. Either way, I'm not taking any chances.

He lifts his hand towards my neck, wicked sharp claws on the tips of his fingers. Panic shoots through me, and I jerk hard to free the candelabra. It pops free, and I swing the heavy piece at Cheshire, aiming for his head. It doesn't get anywhere close to hitting its mark. His fist wraps around it, stopping the metal inches from his face, the grin on his face widening impossibly.

"Be gone, Cheshire!" the Hatter roars as he storms into the room. I assume he's the one who slammed the door open. Why he waited so long to react when Cheshire was clearly threatening me, I don't know. Cheshire fades quickly away, but just before he's gone completely, he speaks.

"Mind the Madness, Clara Bee."

Whatever that means. This entire world is mad.

The Hatter watches me as I set the candelabra back where it came from before turning to face him. He looks exactly the same, his chest still beautifully displayed beneath his jacket. For the first time, I notice a dainty necklace hanging around his neck, but I can't figure out what it is. I do know it draws my eyes to his abs again. I try my hardest not to focus on them.

"Would you like to try and hit me with that, as well?" he asks, his eyes glittering. "I might let you."

He's taking slow, measured steps towards me as I stare at him. More dust swirls around his legs.

"That depends. Do I need to protect myself against you?" I tilt my head slightly, considering his question.

He stops a few feet in front of me, his arms relaxed by his sides.

"You need to protect yourself against everything in Wonderland," he replies. "Especially me."

There's overwhelming sadness in his eyes at the admission, and I find myself leaning towards him, wanting to comfort him.

"Do you intend to hurt me?" I whisper. I had already let my guard down around him, and I'm questioning whether that was the right thing to do or not. He seems so adamant that he is dangerous.

"Sometimes we can't help who we hurt," he says morosely, but then, a wide smile replaces it, spreading across his face. He closes the distance between us until our bodies are flush. I tense, but I don't pull away. My mom would be so exasperated right now. I can hear her voice in my head clearly. *Clara, what have I told you about cozying up to strange men?*

I don't know what it is about the Hatter that makes me trust him. Maybe it's because my job as a lawyer is to help the living while the Hatter helps the dead. Someone evil doesn't help the unfortunate, no matter if it's their job or not. I had seen genuine sadness on his face in that ballroom. Evil people don't care when someone dies. Evil doesn't mourn the passing of strangers. So, I might tense in surprise when he presses his body against mine, but I don't push him away. I might lean closer.

"Do you want me to hurt you?" he asks, his voice husky. "I can make pain feel like pleasure."

"Pain isn't really my thing," I whisper back. My body is growing heated, but I fight the compulsion to wrap my arms around his neck as I look into his gaze. His eyes are such a pretty shade of old gold, sparkling in the dim light of the room. They're like two ancient coins shining in a long forgotten tomb. He studies me intently, and I let him, content to stay close.

"Clara Bee, what are you doing to me? Is this only the prophecy?" he whispers in a sing song voice. I suck in a breath.

"What is the prophecy?" I ask, because I need to know. Everyone keeps talking about it like it's so important. It's obviously a big deal to Wonderland. "How am I supposed to help bring down the Red Queen?"

He smiles, softer this time as he begins to speak. His voice takes on a haunting quality, like it's more than one voice speaking the words coming from his lips.

> "The first of three is Clara Bee
> Who will come to set Wonderland free.
> She'll tame the Hatter and down the Knave
> Because Clara Bee fights for the brave.
> A triad begins to destroy the Queen
> Though nothing is ever easy, it seems.
> She must lose her heart while taking a stand
> To the first son of Wonderland."

As his voice stops, and the haunting quality fades away, I feel the rhyme slipping inside my bones and settling in, like the weight of the words are bearing down on me. My heart gives a hard thud as the Hatter continues to wear that soft smile. Comprehension and shock flood my body when the words register.

"So, you see, Miss Clara Bee." He tilts his head to the side, watching my reaction. "We are destined for each other."

I feel my face harden, his words causing a knee-jerk reaction.

"I make my own destiny," I say, lifting my hands and attempting to push him away. I say attempt because he doesn't actually move. I don't expect the raw strength I can feel in his body, the concealed power under his jacket. I don't expect to like the feel of his chest against my hands.

"Move," I growl, shoving harder.

"Tell me," he says. "Is there a difference between pleasure and pain when your mind is a hurricane?"

I pause, struck by the unbearable sadness in his eyes. Sympathy stalls my hands where they remain against his chest.

"I don't know," I whisper. I know immediately that I've done something wrong.

His face shuts down, his eyes sparking in anger. The old gold color flashes, swirling in metallics.

"I don't need your pity," he snarls before he swings around and storms from the room. I breathe a sigh of relief, clutching my chest to slow my heart rate. The various emotions I just witnessed make my head spin.

When I look at the room again, I realize the entire space is clean, not a speck of dust left. At some point, my nose even stopped itching, and I just hadn't noticed. Everything gleams, sparkling and fresh. There's even a soft lavender smell in the room. I shake my head. I don't even want to question how it had all happened. I'm thankful for it, though.

On the bed, I can see clothing laid out on the purple duvet. As I wander closer, I realize it's a pair of black leather pants and a long, half dress jacket. The top resembles a long coat, the back a full dress that would flow behind me as I walk. From behind, no one would think I'm wearing pants. From the front, I'd look like I'm ready to do business. The jacket has a high neck, a pretty damask design in the purple that closely resembles the Hatter's jacket. Mine is a lighter purple, though not by much. There's a pair of combat boots sitting at the foot of the bed. I raise my eyebrows. The entire outfit is a more feminine version of the Hatter's. Apparently, we're matching now.

If it wasn't so off-putting, it would be cute. Kind of.

Chapter 10

I completely lose track of time in my room. I lay down to take a nap, the trek through the forest catching up with me. I dream of White Rabbits, and rabid flowers reaching forward to take a bite. Someone I can't see, says, "Feed me, Seymour." I wake up disoriented, forgetting where I am for a moment until it all comes rushing back to me. I take a moment to remind myself of everything I know to be true. Eliminate all the illogical possibilities and you're left with the only logical one, right? One, I'm in Wonderland. Two, I'm in the Mad Hatter's house. Three, there's a prophecy written that includes me helping take down the Red Queen. Four, I am not crazy. That about covers it. Somehow, I manage not to freak out.

I stand from the bed, stretching before moving to the window. I push aside the curtains, intending to see how dark it is only to realize the windows have been painted over on the outside. No light comes through at all.

With nothing else to do, I take advantage of the large bathtub. There are vials and pretty bottles full of sweet-smelling liquids and soaps. There's no way to tell which is for bubbles and which is for washing. I end up dumping two different bottles that smell of lavender into the water and hope one of them foams. The result is a bathtub filled with froth so high, I end up turning the water off in a panic. The floor might or might not be dangerous to walk on now. The steam rising from the tub is exactly what I need. When I climb inside and sink into Heaven, it relaxes me in a way I hadn't felt since I landed in Wonderland. I stay in until the water grows cold, and my fingers and toes look like raisins. It's worth it.

Coming from the bathroom, I eye the outfit the Hatter had left for me. I'm tempted to go pick out my own clothing from the wardrobe sitting in the corner, but the outfit intrigues me. It isn't something I would normally wear, usually going for pencil skirts and pant suits, but I've always had this dream of putting on a big dress and running down the hallways like a princess. It isn't the big dress of my dreams, but I bet the flow on that skirt is amazing. I slowly dress in the outfit, taking the time to get used to the leather and the high neck. It definitely fulfills the flowy skirt urge. I feel like a badass, while simultaneously feeling like Cinderella, if Cinderella was a kickass monster hunter. The leather pants really give it some edge. The purple damask jacket-skirt gives it a feminine touch. The combat boots make me feel like I'm going to war, which I suppose, I will be. I'm just finishing wrapping my hair up in a messy bun when there's a knock on the door.

I expect it to be the Hatter. Instead, I'm met by Dormouse staring at me dispassionately. I'm starting to think he's not that much of a fan.

"It's time for tea, Miss Clara," he says before turning and walking away.

I assume I'm supposed to follow him, so I close the door behind me and hurry to catch up. My skirt floats behind me to my utter excitement. Next time, I'm requesting a cape, another thing I've always wanted to wear. Sometimes, I'll wrap my bath towel around my neck and pretend it's a cape while I'm getting ready in the morning. Don't judge. We all want to be a superhero.

Dormouse doesn't say another word as we walk through the maze of hallways until we arrive at the doors to the ballroom again. I turn to tell him thank you, but he's already walking away. Not too friendly, that one. I push open the doors and step inside.

Again, there are a few creatures already sitting at different areas of the table. The first one looks like a giant frog, wearing a coat and tie. As I study him, he looks up and winks at me. I smile at the oddity of it and continue down the room. There's more than last time; I count six. Three look like siblings, all with what looks to me like fox tails and ears.

"Hello, Clara Bee," one rasps.

"Salutations, Clara Bee," another practically yells.

The third sibling only nods as he sips his tea from a dainty tea cup, his pinky in the air like a gentleman. I smile at them sadly, distressed at knowing their fate. I need to ask the Hatter why so many people wind up at his table, but I suspect it's all the Red Queen's doing. It gives me a greater resolve to do what I can for these people, whether the prophecy knows my destiny or not. If I can't help the dead the way the Hatter does, I'm going to damn sure try my best to help the living. It's what I've done my whole life. Why stop now just because I'm in a world only written about in books?

There are two women this time, or females I should say. One looks normal, besides being naked, until I see the tentacles swirling around her, moving teacups around on the table. They leave a slimy film on everything they touch, the way slugs do on my balcony back home. Her smile is wicked when she looks at me, her teeth pointed and serrated like a shark. A film blinks across her eyes. I nod to her, but I don't speak; she gives me the creeps, and to be honest, I'm not sure if she's going to steal my voice or not.

The other woman isn't so much a woman as she is a beast. She's completely covered in fur. She's wearing a pair of slacks and a military style jacket with medals and ribbons pinned to her breast. Her face has a definite wolf look to it while still retaining her human features, giving her a classic horror werewolf appearance. Her fur isn't brown or black, though. She's pure white and utterly beautiful. I have to remind myself not to stare, but I keep flicking back to her clear, blue eyes. They're kind, and it's the reason I feel no fear of her.

"Hello, Ms. Clara Bee." Her voice is like warm honey, and it makes me wish she would just keep speaking. "I've wanted to meet you for a long time. How fortunate I have the pleasure before I move on to the Hereafter."

"Hello," I reply, pausing beside her. She's sitting the closest to the Hatter, only three chairs away.

"I'm Tera." She offers a hand tipped with claws, but I don't hesitate to shake it. Her fur is the softest thing I've ever felt. "It's very nice to meet you."

"I wish it were under different circumstances." I know my voice is sad. Even I can hear the sorrow-tipped words.

"The fact that you are here is reason enough to celebrate. It means the tide will be turning. I may not be here to see it, but I have a family who will. Thank you for fighting for us."

I'm speechless. I've done nothing for Wonderland beside get sucked into a portal. In fact, I was tricked into that, so I've really done zilch. I understand I'm prophesied to be here and to fight for them, but I haven't done a thing for these people. At least, not yet. I intend to do whatever I can to help. If that means taking on the Red Queen, then so be it.

"Come, Clara," the Hatter speaks, rising and striding towards me. He offers me his hand. I slip mine into his and let him lead me towards his seat. The whole time, I fight the emotions threatening to overflow. I make a mental note to ask the Hatter about Tera's family later. I want to see if there's anything I can do for them, to ease the pain they must be going through at her loss.

Once seated, the Hatter takes his chair at the head again and smiles.

"Didn't we just have tea?" I ask. This is the second time, and that's not counting any I might have missed before the last one. I didn't realize it's something that happens more than once every so often. Once or twice a month, maybe. Once a week, a possibility. But every single day? That seems extreme. The fact that there has been a decent number of people at both parties worries me.

"It's always tea time," the Hatter replies solemnly. I don't comment. Instead, I make a vow to change it and save the people I'm able to. "You must be starving." The Hatter sounds way too excited about that fact, like he can't wait to see me eat. If I was a nice normal girl like my mom always wanted, I would have been weirded out. Instead, I smile at his exuberance.

He snaps his fingers, and food appears on the table in front of me, a plate piled high with sweet-looking cakes and croissants. There's a jam on the side that smells like Heaven and strawberries. My stomach growls loudly, and I realize I haven't eaten since breakfast at the office. How long ago had that been? It was normal for me to forget to eat through the day when I had a lot of work to do. Has it only been a day or two?

Even though my stomach gives another thunderous growl, I hesitate.

"Should I be eating this?" I ask the Hatter, staring at the plate with longing. I'm pretty sure White mentioned a rule about food and that I shouldn't be eating anything. The Hatter doesn't answer me. He leans back in his chair, hanging one leg over the arm, spread eagled in a way that displays every inch of his body. He smirks when my eyes drop. "You said I shouldn't trust you," I point out. His smile widens.

"Take a gamble, take a bite. Is he trustworthy or is he not?" he sings.

The frog creature laughs as he digs into his plate. When I look closely, I can see his croissants are topped with flies. He's slurping, and the sounds are entirely disgusting, but I'm growing accustomed to Wonderland. It doesn't even give me pause. The other guests all have food tailored to their diets. I notice Tera's has raw meat in between the slices of bread. I don't ask what kind of meat it is for fear of the answer.

"I don't know to trust you or not, but I accept your gamble with some thought," I sing, mimicking his rhyming.

His eyes light up, and he straightens in his chair, leaning forward, as I take a bite of what I think is a Danish. The flavor explodes on my tongue, the taste unlike anything I've ever eaten before. I had thought the tea tasted like Ambrosia. The food makes the tea taste like ash. I moan as I take another bite, feeling my hunger take over. The Hatter watches me, enraptured as I begin to systematically clean the plate set before me.

It's not until I've finished most of the food that I realize something is off, that I don't feel right. There's a buzzing under my skin, a crawling sensation that is usually the first sign I've had too much alcohol. The skin under my fingernails, and deep inside my ear canals where I can never possibly scratch, itches. Suddenly hot, I look at the Hatter in question.

"Was there something in the food?" I ask. With my own ears, I can tell my words are a bit slurred. Then I giggle. I roll my eyes internally. I'm such a predictable drunk. Soon, I'll be dancing on the table and laughing hysterically over nothing.

"All the food in Wonderland has side effects." The Hatter watches in amusement as I start to sway in my seat. Music fills the room—I have no idea from where—and I can't stop myself from moving to the deep, pulsing beat. I can feel it in my toes, working its way through my body.

"I feel drunk," I say, giggling. "Like really drunk." Like, I'm pretty sure I'm going to be hurting tomorrow if this is anything like drinking twelve shots of tequila back to back.

"You're beautiful." The Hatter smiles with the words, and I suddenly feel as beautiful as he sees me. I feel like I can take on the world at this very moment and win.

"You might want to stop eating," Tera says from beside me. "Or else you'll wake up tomorrow without your memories."

I turn to her sharply, my senses clearing for a moment, long enough to meet her eyes. I trust her to tell me the truth, and I somehow know she isn't lying. Some gut instinct tells me she couldn't lie to me if she wanted to.

"I'll forget my memories?"

"Only if you have so much that you black out," she clarifies, smiling. "So, I'd suggest slowing down."

I push the plate away, the few crumbs on the plate calling to me. In the moment of sobriety, I flip the plate upside down, hiding the leftover pieces. The Hatter chuckles but doesn't comment. The intense buzzing comes back with a vengeance, the music sending vibrations through my body until I can't help but sway in my seat again, laughing along with the other guests as they toss playful banter back and forth.

"You couldn't handle me," Tera growls at the fox brothers, sniffing disdainfully at them. It's the first time I'm seen her anything but kind, and it reminds me that she resembles a wolf more than a woman.

"Perhaps," one of the brothers answers. "But you also can't handle us."

"What makes you think I would entertain that thought?"

I listen in on the conversation, enraptured with the turn of events. With a nice buzz going, I can't control the word vomit that tumbles out.

"Just kiss each other already!" I clamp my hand over my mouth in surprise.

Tera looks over at me, her eyes dancing with a fire that's as hot as the tension in the room. Then she throws back her head and laughs. The fox brothers join in. I watch, fascinated as Tera stands from her chair before stepping up and onto the table.

"Join me, Clara Bee." She reaches out to me. I slip my fingers into her claw-tipped hand, and she hoists me onto the table with no effort. "Let's dance."

Back at home, I had been to the club with my girlfriends. I hadn't done it since my college days, but I still remember the fun of pulling each other onto the dance floor and dancing together, drawing every eye in the room. This was kind of like that, only better.

Tera pulls me against her, and we begin to sway, her fuzzy tail swishing around my legs as we twirl. I laugh as dishes clatter off the tables and go crashing to the floor. Hatter smiles at us, completely at ease as he sips his tea. The frog moves over to the tentacle woman and sits beside her. They lean their heads together and talk, smiling at Tera and I as we sway to music. I have no idea where the upbeat song is coming from, but I don't question it. I feel way too good for all that overthinking.

The fox brothers stand up from their seats as one. They leap onto the table, wicked smiles on their faces as they approach Tera. She faces off against them as I sway my hips and spin in circles atop the table. Thank goodness it's a sturdy one. It would have been mortifying to fall off.

My attention is riveted on Tera and the fox brothers who begin to sway together in a sensual dance. The brothers surround her, slipping in sly touches here and there that would normally make my face flame. In the state I'm in now, I enjoy the show. I can't seem to look away for a few moments until I feel the heat of another gaze on me. I turn and meet the flashing golden eyes of the Hatter. He isn't watching Tera and the brothers. He only has eyes for me.

The song switches to something deep and sensual, the base notes pounding hard enough to travel through the table and into my body. I keep my eyes on the Hatter, taking him all in. He's sitting in his chair still, leaning back lazily, one leg hanging over the arm again in a way that displays him completely. My body keeps swaying, my hips moving to the rhythm. I move towards him slowly, stepping over dishes that rattle with the bass. I kick a few dishes from the table when I judge the distance wrong, the fuzziness making me stumble a bit. Hatter straightens in his chair when I come to the edge, looking down on him. I gingerly kneel down and sit, spreading my legs on either side of him to dangle over the ledge. He grins at my position, his hands wrapping around my ankles before trailing up my leather-clad legs to cup the back of my knees.

"What can I help you with, Ms. Clara Bee?" he asks. His voice is deep and husky, going right through me and into my core. A heat spreads low in my belly as I inhale the scent of chocolate and Chamomile tea.

Instead of answering, I lean forward slightly. The Hatter's eyes drop to my lips, and I smile. I'm sure he expects something sexy, maybe a breathy whisper or a saucy pick-up line. What do I do instead in my drunken stupor? I boop him on the nose, giggling when a look of surprise crosses his face. I pluck the top hat from his head and settle it on mine, the messy bun having fallen out a long time ago. My hair is currently down and a frizzy mess, but it doesn't bother me. Hatter growls at me for stealing his hat, a sexy sound that makes my breasts tighten. I'm pretty sure I just committed a big no-

no. Did White tell me not to touch the Hatter's top hat? I don't remember. When the Hatter takes me in, sitting spread around him, laughter on my face, and the top hat on my head, his expression softens, the danger in his eyes disappearing as fast as it had come. His hands tighten on the backs of my knees before pulling me towards him. I slide from the edge of the table and land with an oomph on his lap. The top hat stays perched on my head.

Beneath me, I can feel his arousal pushing through his leather pants, and the heady sense of feeling wanted rushes through me. I'm glad I'm not alone with this overwhelming attraction; the Hatter seems just as affected as I am. Our eyes lock, pulling each other in, his gold wrapping around me and swirling with my grey. Everything else fades away, the laughter, the music, the other guests. There's only the Hatter and me.

"I believe I owe you a kiss," I whisper, my voice husky as I lean forward.

His face grows serious before I close my eyes, preparing for the kiss I'm sure will rock my world. My only hope is that I'm sober enough to remember it. I feel his hands clench at my waist, and I realize just how intimate we are being in a room full of other people. It doesn't deter me at all. If anything, I feel more aroused because of it, that the Hatter feels no shame, no worry for me or my performance. I might be a bit drunk on Wonderland food, but that doesn't mean I don't know what's happening. I'm lingering there, damn near puckering my lips, but nothing happens. I open my eyes in confusion to the Hatter's still serious face.

"No." His voice is hard as he studies my face. "I want you to be wholly yourself when we kiss."

Embarrassment floods my body for the first time, and I feel my cheeks heat. In the state I'm in now, the rejection hits me hard, growing with every drunken breath I take. Tears threaten to fall even though I know I'm overreacting. My mortification has no logic behind it, and yet, it hits me like a ton of bricks.

The Hatter's gaze stutters when he sees the tear that slips over my cheek. I dash it away in horror and clamber from his lap. I'm about as graceful as a one-legged flamingo, but I make it off without embarrassing myself further. For the first time, I notice the music is gone, and I wonder if it's my doing or the Hatter's. The other guests are staring at me. Tera climbs down from the table, reaching for me. She wraps her arms around me in a hug, and it's exactly what I need.

"It's okay," she whispers in my ear. "It's just the food. It heightens our emotions. Go. Take some time to breath. You'll feel better."

"Thank you," I reply, a sob in my voice. If I don't get out of here, I'm going to lose my shit. I squeeze her hand. "For everything."

"No, thank you, Miss Clara. I'll see you again. Stay strong now. The Hatter, he's a creature of Wonderland. The land is hurting, so he suffers. You must stay strong against his madness."

I smile, give her another quick hug, and leave, my skirt billowing out behind me. If I wasn't so distraught, I would have been excited about that fact. I don't turn around and look at the Hatter. I forget I'm wearing his top hat.

I step out through the doors of the ballroom, the effects of the food wearing off almost instantly. I take a deep breath, the emotions from a few seconds ago almost disappearing. There's still the sting of rejection there, barely, but I'm able to ignore and rationalize how pointless it was to feel that way. The Hatter was being a gentleman and had enough honor to not take advantage. I should respect that instead of wishing I already knew what his lips taste like. Either the food only has the effect in the ballroom or I embraced the buzzed feeling a little too much. It wears off so fast, I'm left standing outside the ballroom, rubbing my forehead in confusion.

I'm turning back towards the ballroom, preparing myself to apologize to the Hatter when there's a loud knock on the front door. I stare, but I don't move forward. No way am I answering a door in Wonderland by myself. The knock comes again, more insistent, and angry. There's so much anger in that knock that the door rattles hard. I worry it'll just be knocked down completely, but it stands its ground, keeping out whoever is behind it. When the pounding gets so loud I can feel it through the marble floors, I rush up the stairs and around the corner, pushing my back against the wall. I peek around the edge just as Dormouse steps out. There's worry on his face, the first emotion I've seen from him, and it's that sight that sends me into a panic. If Dormouse is worried, then something is definitely wrong.

I hear a muffled shout on the other side, accompanied with someone hitting the door as hard as they can. All the warmth is sucked from the air. I hold my breath as Dormouse reaches for the knob.

Chapter 11

Dormouse hesitates when a crack forms on the door, the anger radiating through the door growing to nuclear levels. I hover in my hiding spot, my hands clenching onto the banister as I lean over to see who's there. When Dormouse begins backing away from the door, I let out my breath and fight to get my racing heart under control. Something is happening, and I'm debating between taking off into the maze of hallways and rushing down the stairs to the Hatter, hopefully, beating whoever is behind that door.

A hand lands on my shoulder, and I jump as it spins me around. I bring my arm up, ready to cold cock whoever has the nerve to touch me, but I relax when I realize it's only Cheshire. I shouldn't. Cheshire is just as threatening as whoever is on the other side of the door, but he's the lesser of two evils right now. I know what to expect from him. The person behind the door? Not so much.

"Come with me." He tugs on my arm, trying to get me to move. "We have to go. Now."

"Who is it?" I ask, because, sure, I'm freaked out, but I'm also incredibly curious. I should be running, screaming my head off to get away from the door. I have a sudden flare of horror. "It's not a Bandersnatch, is it?"

Cheshire snorts and shakes his head. "The Knave knows you're here. That's him trying to break down the door."

He yanks to get me moving, pulling me down a hallway away

from the commotion. I can barely keep up with his long stride, double timing my steps in an attempt to.

"The Knave finding me is bad, right?"

"The Knave belongs to the Red Queen. If he finds you, he'll take you to her." He looks back at me, more serious than I had yet to see him. "She will kill you, slowly and brutally until you beg for mercy that she'll never show you."

I swallow the choking fear that climbs my throat. I had already vowed to help these people. I won't back down at the first sign of trouble. I can only assume things will get worse before they can get better. I have no time for fear.

"Why don't we just fight the Knave?" I ask. "Why are we running if I'm supposed to take him down?"

Cheshire looks back at me again and grins.

"Who says we're running?"

Finally, Cheshire pulls me to a stop outside a door. I can no longer hear the banging, but if I focus, I think I can feel a deep thumping through the floors. I have no idea how any of the house guests find their way around the maze of hallways. I try my hardest to note the directions we take, only to lose track after the twelfth turn. The house doesn't look that big from the outside. On the inside, it might as well be as big as it wants, going on and on as if there's no end.

Cheshire kicks open the door and storms inside, dragging me behind him. I'm starting to see a pattern with Wonderland men, but I don't worry about it right now. Instead, my jaw drops.

The room is massive, but that's not what surprises me. Every wall is completely covered with weapons, displayed from floor to ceiling. There are so many types, I can feel my brain literally explode from overload. One wall is covered in all kinds of guns, from tiny innocent-looking things to something I'm sure must be a rocket launcher. It looks pretty close to the ones I've seen in movies at home, but the barrel isn't straight. It's curved for whatever reason.

Another wall is filled with various types of swords and knives. I'm tempted to arm myself with a wicked-looking battle ax I see, one befitting my spider-killing battle cry, but I doubt I could lift it if I wanted to. The other two walls are filled with items I have no names for. I can't even describe some of the things to guess. Cheshire walks over to the gun wall and studies the choices, shaking his head slightly when he looks past particular ones.

"Can you fight?" His voice carries across the room, but he doesn't turn to look at me.

I shake my head even though he can't see. "I've had some self-defense classes, and I took the CHL class, so I can carry my gun, but that's it." A fact I'm regretting now.

"We'll have to fix that," he replies with his back still turned to me. He reaches high on the wall and plucks a gun much bigger than anything I have ever handled. "At least, you know how to fire a gun."

"Uh, is there any way you have a 9mm?"

The gun is huge, a mix between a handgun and the Uzis the old time gangsters used to carry. It has a large chamber underneath it, which I think holds bullets. The barrel of the gun is long and definitely larger than the little handgun I carry in my briefcase when I'm not in court. The thing has to have gigantic bullets, and I have no idea what caliber they can be. They'll probably have a name like "Three Parts Past" or "Half past dead". Cheshire brings it over. When I look closer at the barrel of the gun, I can see the words "Heart breaker" etched as a red filigree design. I raise my eyebrows. A bit on the nose with that name. Cheshire hands it to me carelessly, and I panic when the firearm almost falls from my hands.

"This is Wonderland." Cheshire begins strapping all manner of weapons onto his body. He's sliding swords into sheaths across his back and long daggers in thigh holders. I watch, holding the gun cautiously. "A 9mm won't do anything here but piss people off."

"Noted." I roll my eyes. Of course, I'd have to shoot bullets meant to take down a dinosaur in Wonderland. It makes sense in an illogical way.

I see him stash an armory's worth of weapons in his clothes, using every pocket and adding some when that doesn't seem to be enough. Finally, he turns to me and looks me up and down. He kneels and reaches for my thigh. I take a hasty step out of reach. He looks up at me and cocks an eyebrow.

"I don't exactly trust you," I point out.

"You shouldn't." He grins at me. "I'm only trying to strap some weapons to your thighs." He gestures for me to move closer. "May I?"

I nod hesitantly, taking a step forward. He grabs my leg, his hands clinical as he begins buckling some straps around my thigh tightly. He's mechanical, nothing sensual about the act, and it sets me at ease. After strapping sheaths to both of my thighs, he slides a pair of beautiful long knives into them before standing. He grabs another leather belt and fits it around my waist, pulling it tight enough that it won't slide when I'm moving. There's a fancy holster for the Heart Breaker, another strap on it that wraps around the top of my thigh, securing it. The gun is heavy when he slides it inside. On the other side of my waist, there's a scabbard attached. A short sword goes in there. I have no idea how to use the sword or the knives, and I'm hoping I won't have to. That's probably wishful thinking, though. When he's finished, it feels like I've been tied up without actually restricting me. I also feel like a badass, even if I have no idea how to use any of it.

Cheshire steps back and studies me before grabbing two small throwing knives from the wall and sliding them into the sides of my combat boots.

"There." He nods his head. "Now you look like you're prepared for war." He begins to walk away, towards the door. "Only shoot the Knave or the Queen's Cards. And then, only if you have to."

"How do I tell the difference between the bad guys and friendlies?" I ask. Because this is Wonderland. I have no idea what the Knave or the Cards look like. What if they look like the other creatures?

"You'll know," Cheshire growls, disdain dripping from his voice. Okay, wow. No love lost there.

Cheshire throws open the door, and fear spikes through me.

"Where is the Hatter? And White?" I ask, suddenly remembering they are in the house, too.

"White is off doing whatever he does. The Hatter is answering the door and showing them to the tea room," he answers, that sinister grin spreading across his face. At least, the books have that right. Cheshire's grin is downright scary.

We slip out of the room. I stay as close as possible to Cheshire as we creep along the hallway quietly. Everything is silent, throwing the house into a more eerie atmosphere than usual. Normally, there's a chatter in the halls from creatures I can't see, and the house groans. It seems even the house knows it needs to be quiet. I try to mimic the soundless steps that Cheshire takes, but I'm just not as stealthy as a cat. My outfit swishes, and with each step, some of the buckles on me give off a soft jingle. Every now and then, a floorboard creaks under my combat boots, and I cringe, hoping no one is around that means us harm. Each time it happens, I see Cheshire's shoulder tense, and I know he's fighting hard not to get annoyed.

We come to the end of a hallway, nowhere to go but to turn right. Cheshire holds up his hand, telling me to stop without saying anything. I immediately go into fight mode, which pretty much just means my hands flutter around my body wondering which weapon I should grab. Did I mention I have no idea what I'm doing? I can argue my way out of anything, wielding words like weapons. Actual weapons? One CHL class. I know the basics, but I'm probably not a sharpshooter. If it comes to a battle, I could become a liability more than a help. That won't stop me from actually trying to help, though.

We stand poised at the end of the hallway, Cheshire's ears flicking back and forth, for a few minutes. I keep my breathing slow and measured, just in case something can hear them.

"Wait here," Cheshire whispers so low, I have to strain for the words. He slips around the corner silently.

I wait, and wait, but when he doesn't return after long minutes, I grow antsy. I pull the gun from my waist; it's really my safest option for weapons. I'm likely to chop my own arm off with a sword. I hope the safety works the same way as my gun back home. I ready myself, keeping my shoulder relaxed and my arms steady as I grip the odd gun tightly. I take a deep breath and peek my head around the wall.

I should have run earlier.

I stumble backwards, damn near tripping over the back of my outfit in an attempt to get back. I don't scream, but only because I'm so surprised, nothing escapes my throat. As I back away, the man who had been waiting around the corner steps fully around the wall. He zeroes in on me as I get my first clear look of the Knave. Cheshire is right. There's no way I could mistake him for anyone else.

He's wearing golden armor, glistening and perfect, a mockery against the deeds he carries out for the Red Queen. There's a giant red heart on the breast, emblazoned for all to see, to show who owns him. There's a wound on the left side of his chest, like someone had once ripped out his heart. In the bloody and ripped flesh, tiny red roses blossom, there for everyone to see. The left side of his face suffers a similar fate. Where his eye used to be, there's a gaping hole filled with more roses springing forth. I can tell he probably used to be handsome. He has a square jaw and a strong nose. His remaining eye is brilliant blue, his hair a faded blond. There's a tiny black heart inked beneath the remaining eye. His face looks mottled and beaten, blood and scars marking the pale skin. With trembling hands, I raise the gun, aiming it right at his chest. He doesn't even flinch.

"And who might you be, Pretty Thing?" he asks, a grimace on his face. I'm pretty sure he means the grimace as a smile, but it comes across strained. The left side of his face doesn't seem to work anymore. His voice though, is beautiful. It's deep and resonate, and I wonder at the contradiction between that and his appearance.

For each slow step he takes towards me, I back away, not wanting to be anywhere close to him. I don't respond to his question, keeping the gun trained on him. He doesn't seem worried at all about the Heart Breaker but his face morphs into rage when I continue to move away from him.

"I said who are you?" he yells, slamming his fist against the wall beside him. I flinch, but I don't jump, a win in my book.

"Stop!" Hatter shouts, striding up behind him. He passes the Knave and comes right up to me, threading my arm in his. He swiftly grabs the gun from my hand and tucks it back into the holster, the action so fast, I barely follow it. "She's from my tea party. A guest."

He plucks the top hat from my head that I'm somehow still wearing. It hadn't even felt like I'd been wearing a hat at all.

"I've never seen her in Wonderland," the Knave says, that grimace on his face. "And I've never seen a guest wielding a gun and wearing your top hat."

"Don't you think I'd know if she wasn't part of Wonderland?" Hatter shrugs. "The dead are dead whether they lost their head or lost their heart."

The Knave doesn't move for a moment. Then, his eye narrows, and I have to fight the gulp in my throat. I try to mimic the peaceful look the tea party guests all have, but it's difficult. I'm positive I don't have the aura of peace around me, a staple for sitting at the Hatter's table. I'm battling my fight or flight response. I equally want to pull the gun from its holster and blow the Knave to smithereens just as much as I want to turn tail and run, getting as far away from the man as possible. The only things that keep me standing here are my vow to help Wonderland and the Hatter's arm in mine.

"You don't mind if I watch you cross her over then, do you." It should have been a question, but the Knave isn't asking. It's a command.

Inside, I'm freaking out, screaming. Externally, the only sign of my discomfort is how tightly I'm holding onto the Hatter. My other hand is shaking, but I tuck it against my back and out of sight.

"It's a very intimate occasion," the Hatter says, and I understand what he's trying to do. Get rid of the Knave. Get his attention off of me.

The Knave slams his fist against the wall again. This time, a large crack spider webs across the wall, originating where his hand craters.

"I will see you cross her," he snarls.

The Hatter frowns, but nods his head solemnly. Hatter tugs on my arm, leading me down the hallway. When we pass by the Knave, he takes a deep sniff at the air, like he's scenting me. I force myself not to react as we move by. We float down the stairs—I stumble a few times, but the Hatter keeps a firm grip on me—as the Knave follows behind us. The Hatter is seemingly unperturbed by anything that is happening. Me, I'm panicking inside. How the hell are we going to get out of this one?

When we enter the ballroom, I'm happy to see there aren't any other creatures in the area. I don't know where they are, if they crossed over already or are hiding out of sight, or how the Hatter took care of it. Small blessings. I don't know if the Knave can hurt people that are already dead, but I'd rather not find out. The fact that they escaped makes me relax just a little bit more. The shaking in my hand stops.

I glance behind me in time to see a few . . . things join the Knave from nowhere. They have to be the Queen's Cards that Cheshire warned me about. Again, there's no mistaking them for anything else. They're grotesque creatures, standing tall like men. They must have been people at some point, but that's all I can tell. They have no faces, just a blank slate where they should have eyes, mouth and nose. They're wearing metal helmets, each stamped with a different suit of cards. They stride forward with swagger, either completely confident or nonplussed. I have no idea how they see where they're going. They each carry some sort of club or bat with wicked-looking nails sticking from them. The clubs are covered in blood and bits of gore, like no one ever cleans them. As I stare at them, the one in front's face shifts. Instead of the blank stretch of skin, a mouth opens, taking up the entire space. It's full of sharp, dripping teeth. They're stained red. I turn back forward again so fast, my eyes blur. No way do I want anything to do with those things. Give me Beezles any day.

I try my hardest to breathe normally as Hatter leads us past the table and to the back of the room where the trees and mushrooms grow thickest. He hesitates a moment before throwing his hat on the ground in front of us. A swirling portal opens up, sucking strands of my hair free and whipping around me. I draw a sharp breath in, remembering the last time I went through a portal. I blacked out the first time. Would I do the same with this one? Hatter tightens my arm in his, keeping a firm grasp on me.

"Well?" The Knave is standing behind us with his arms crossed over his chest. A few delicate rose petals fall to the ground.

The Hatter leans close. "Don't let go of me," he whispers.

"Okay," I whisper back, grabbing on tight. I get the feeling we're about to do something that hasn't been done before. I'm about to enter the Hereafter, where the dead go. Is it like Heaven or like Hell? I don't have time to ask.

"Do you trust me?" Hatter asks, taking a step closer to the portal. I move forward with him, the gravity beginning to pull at my clothes.

I reach up and use my other hand to grasp his coat sleeve. I need all the security I can get.

"Yes," I breathe, my voice shaking a bit.

The Hatter looks at me, his eyes glittering. There's a small curl to his lips, like he's enjoying this a bit too much, like insanity is on the tip of his tongue.

"Then let's go on an adventure," he whoops, and we step through the portal.

Chapter 12

As we pass through the portal, I struggle not to close my eyes against the bright colors swirling around us. When I had fallen through White's rabbit hole, it had been a vortex of green and white, the same colors the sneaky bastard seems to favor. Hatter's portal is a mixture of gold, purple, and black, dragging me in until my eyes burn with the effort it takes to keep them open.

I battle the rising panic as we seem to move faster and faster through the colors. The only thing keeping me from completely losing my sanity is the Hatter beside me, his arm threading through mine, his strength locking us together. I almost chuckle at that, as inappropriate a time it is, that the Mad Hatter is keeping me sane. What are the odds of that?

When I think it will just keep on going forever— the Hereafter must be a long journey— the colors dissipate, and we step out into a lush, green jungle. The air is damp, immediately making my clothes feel ten times more suffocating. The high collar is the worst, but the leather pants are close behind. Everything is dripping with moisture, almost like it has just rained, just enough to make it more humid. I tug at the collar of my jacket, hating my entire outfit that seems perfect for Wonderland but is terrible for the sweltering Hereafter.

I look around us, the sounds of the jungle reaching my ears. Birds call to each other in the trees, the screech of a monkey sounds close by. None of them make my ears bleed. It's exactly what I imagined Wonderland would be, a magical, peaceful world, the sun shining bright and filtering through the trees. Not surprising, I was a hundred percent wrong.

The Hatter doesn't say anything as I study the new world I find myself in. Again, I shake my head. I'll definitely end up in the nuthouse if I tell anyone back home about all this. With his arm still locked around mine, he reaches behind him to where the portal is still swirling. He snatches his hat from the floor on the other side, and it confuses me. We just traveled for long minutes to reach the Hereafter, and yet, I'm able to see back into the ballroom where the Knave stands. Anger clouds his once handsome face as he watches us. It makes the roses quiver. I can't believe that even though the trip through the portal seemed like it took forever, that we can still see through to the other side. I watch as the Hatter plops his hat back on his head. The portal begins to close, shrinking smaller and smaller. The Hatter flicks the Knave the bird, a smirk on his face. The portal closes on the Knave's scream of rage.

"So, this is the Hereafter?" What else can I really say? I just stepped through a Wonderland portal into their version of the Afterlife. I like to think I'm handling the situation pretty well when everything I thought I knew has been turned on its head.

"Yes," the Hatter replies, looking down at me. "And you shouldn't be here. This place is meant for the dead."

"But you're here," I point out. I know for a fact he is very much alive. He's as solid as I am. His arm hasn't loosened one bit, and I get the feeling he doesn't know what will happen if he isn't touching me. He's much more tense than he had been in Wonderland.

"I am neither here nor there."

"What does that even mean?"

"A son of Wonderland cannot die unless the end of Wonderland is nigh," he sings, tipping his head towards me.

"So, if Wonderland dies, you die," I clarify. He nods his head once. "And that's what's happening now?"

"The Red Queen is a plague upon our world, draining it even as she grows stronger." He looks into the distance, sadness on his face. "Alice should have never taken the throne."

I stop abruptly, my feet refusing to take another step. The Hatter makes a comical dramatic stop you only see in cartoons, like I anchored him down. I know he's much stronger than me. He did it on purpose, and it makes me smile briefly before I bring up the topic again.

"The Red Queen is The Alice?" I ask, because who saw that coming? Isn't Alice supposed to be a twelve-year-old innocent girl?

His eyes darken, anger moving across his face before fading away.

"A story for another time, I'm afraid," he answers, meeting my eyes. "We're on a time limit."

"What kind of time limit?"

"I've never brought someone living to the Hereafter and you're already starting to fade. We need to get to the other portal and get you out of here. The Knave will no doubt be waiting at this one."

"I'm not fading." I look down at my body and nearly choke on my words. The hand not holding onto the Hatter is translucent, looking more like a fairy's gossamer wings than skin. "Oh, shit!"

He tugs until we're moving again. I stumble after him, staring at my vanishing hand.

"Come along, Clara Bee. It's not your time yet."

"What happens if I fade completely?" I ask, my voice a rough whisper.

"No need to worry." He smiles. "You said you trusted me."

"But what happens if I fade in the Hereafter?"

He glances at me from the corner of his eyes. There's sadness there, a glimmer sparkling in them.

"Then you disappear completely. It would be like you never existed."

I can feel the horror cross my face, the idea freaking me out more than anything else I have encountered so far. Prophesied to defeat the Red Queen, nothing. Destined to be the Mad Hatter's mate, okay. Disappear like I never existed, hell no!

The Hatter scoffs and leans down, scooping me up bridal style. I squeak as the world tilts, and I wrap my arms around the Hatter's neck in panic. He wiggles his eyebrows as his arms gets very cozy around me.

"You're moving too slowly," he shrugs. "Clara Bee was meant for me, and I can't let her die. So, hold on tight, Miss Clara Bee, and everything will be alright," he sings.

And then he begins to run, the jungle flying by at a speed that leaves me breathless. This time, I close my eyes against the blurring colors.

Everything looks the same to me. Green, green, green with various pops of color from the floral vines. The sounds don't change, a constant chitter of birds and animals rustling through the undergrowth. Not a single bug tries to bite me. The Hereafter is blessedly free of blood sucking insects and tiny poisonous things.

We come across a stream, and the Hatter slows. There's sweat dripping down his face and chest, his hair is sticking to his forehead. I'm pretty sure my hair is a rat's nest. Sweat slicked and tangled isn't one of my sexier looks. The Hatter sets me down, his hand coming down to wrap around mine, making sure our skin is always touching. Both of our palms are clammy, but neither one of us comments on it.

"Are you thirsty?" The Hatter looks at the water longingly.

I take stock of my body. My entire arm is faded but nothing else is. Perhaps, it isn't progressing as fast as the Hatter fears. I take a moment to think about it, but the decision is made for me when my hand moves to my collar and begins undoing the buttons down my coat. Hatter looks at me in puzzlement.

"I'm too hot," I supply as an answer while I pull one arm free of the heavy jacket, switching the hand holding onto the Hatter's before pulling off the other sleeve. The jacket drops to the ground, the leaves stirring with the heavy weight.

"We don't have time." Hatter shakes his head, but he watches as I pull the sweat-slicked cami up and over my head that I had been wearing underneath. The different weapons harnesses are next. They clatter to the ground, the metal buckles clanking together.

"It isn't moving that fast. It won't take long. I just want to cool down." I kick the combat boots off and start working on my leather pants. Unbuttoning them with only one hand proves difficult, but I eventually manage the feat. "Now, are you going to join me or just sit on the edge? Either way, I'm getting in that water."

I peel the leather pants off, the sweat making them suction to me. It won't be fun getting into them again, but at least, I have a moment where I can feel a cool breeze on my heated skin. I might consider walking the rest of the way like this, dressed only in my bra and underwear. Hatter doesn't seem to mind. In fact, he doesn't seem to be able to take his eyes off me.

I tug on his hand.

"Well?" He takes barely a second before he whips off his top hat and sets it on the ground beside him. His jacket follows. I watch as more and more skin is revealed, waiting expectantly for his pants to follow.

"I'll leave these on." He kicks his boots off, but doesn't remove his leather.

"Are you sure? That doesn't seem comfortable." There's no way I would swim in the leather pants.

He grins.

"Tempting fate would be great except you still owe a kiss. If I lost my pants, I'd lose my chance, to touch lips to lips."

I return the smile.

"Suit yourself, My Dear Hatter, if that's really what you're about. But I hope you know exactly what you're missing out," I sing back as I dip my toe in the water. It's cold but not freezing. I step inside, sighing as my body slowly adjusts to the temperature change. I glance back at Hatter, grinning. He's still standing on the edge, a soft smile on his face. "What?"

"I like when you do that," he replies softly, his fingers gently squeezing mine.

"Do what?" I'm genuinely confused. I hadn't done anything out of the ordinary.

"Embrace my madness."

My heart gives a hard throb in my chest when I hear the emotion in his voice. I pull on the Hatter's arm until he's forced to step into the water with me. He's taller than me, so our faces aren't level, but I make sure he's paying attention as I look up into his eyes. I wrap him in a hug, a bit of an awkward one with our hands linked together, but I hug him as hard as I can. He smells like his normal Chocolate and Chamomile, an enticing mixture that makes me inhale deeply.

"Hatter," I whisper, drawing his eyes to mine. "You are more than just your madness. And you are perfect. Don't ever think I won't accept who you are."

He frowns.

"You don't mind the madness? My mind is a very dark place."

"If I minded, do you think I would be standing here in my underwear thinking about how your lips taste? Or that you're the most interesting person I have ever met?"

Hatter lifts me into the air suddenly, his arms wrapped around me, tightening our hug. I laugh as he steps further into the stream, the cool water rushing past our thighs. Then he squats down until only our heads stick out. I instantly feel better, the stream is exactly what I need.

"Clara Bee," Hatter sighs as he leans his forehead against mine.

"Can we kiss now?" I ask, anticipating the moment, but he shakes his head.

"We can't linger long. You're still fading."

I look down at my arm to see that my shoulder is transparent now. I groan.

"Clara!" a voice calls from the bank. "What in Wonderland are you doing here?"

I jerk my head towards the sound, my eyes falling on Tera. She's dressed in a green robe, a towel thrown over her shoulder. When I glance behind her, I can see the fox brothers making their way towards us, all dressed in similar green robes. So, they did make it to the Hereafter. I wonder how even as I raise my eyebrows and smile.

"Tera!" I bite my lip. "It's a long story. And apparently, we don't have much time." I raise my arm for her to see, and her eyes widen in panic.

"You need to get out of the Hereafter right away!"

"We plan to. I wasn't dressed for a jungle, so the heat got a little unbearable."

Tera eyes my state of undress before flicking to the Hatter who I'm wrapped around like a spider monkey.

"Looks to me you had the same idea we did," she laughs, the sound husky. "The boys and I were just about to go skinny dipping."

I smile even as I blush. She seems happy, and that makes me happier for her. I have no idea what her life was like in Wonderland, what hardships she had to face that eventually led to her death, but here, she's carefree and safe. I feel much better after seeing her.

"We have to go, Clara Bee," Hatter whispers in my ear. Part of my chest is fading, and I stand up abruptly, pulling Hatter with me. We climb from the stream and start dressing. I have to do a little hop dance to get the pants back on. I was right. Putting them on again does suck. The jacket is worse, like buttoning myself up in a heating blanket. I leave most of the buttons undone in an attempt to stop some of the heat.

When I finish, Tera hugs me to her.

"Stay strong. And watch out for the Knave."

"Oh, we've met," I reply. "That's how we ended up here." Hatter picks me up again. "Have fun with the boys!"

"Have fun with the Hatter!" She winks at me as we take off, faster than before.

I have a quick view of the Fox brothers pulling the robe from Tera's shoulders before they're out of sight.

When the Hatter finally begins to slow down, my head feels as light as my body. I look down at myself, everything I can see is translucent, resembling a ghost more than a person, and I frown. I try not to let the panic take hold when the Hatter's arms tighten around me and worry creases his face. I have no idea how to deal with what is happening, how to fight against it. How do I stop myself from blinking out of existence? Get the hell out of Dodge, is the only thing that comes to mind.

"How much further?" My voice sounds different, more breathy and soft, like it's fading away, too.

"Not much. Not much," Hatter replies. He keeps repeating the words over and over again under his breath. It does nothing to soothe my nerves.

We break through the tree line, stepping into a circle of trees, a clearing. In the center, blending into the green of the jungle, stands a bit of Wonderland. Giant mushrooms stand tall and proud in the center, forming an archway as they bend together. Wonderland bugs flutter around the small area, buzzing incessantly. They fly around lazily, the complete opposite of the attack mode they seem to be set on normally. The sound of birds and animals is absent here, the place having a holy feeling to it.

The Hatter doesn't hesitate. He strides right up the giant mushrooms, purpose in his steps. The bugs buzz faster, realizing we're here, but they don't touch us. Right at the doorway, he sets me down gently, keeping one arm firmly twisted with mine. I sway when my feet touch the ground, unnerved when I realize I can't feel them. It mostly feels like I'm floating, kind of like that one time Jill Landon convinced me to smoke a joint in high school. The ground hums beneath me, a dragging sensation pulling on my body. I don't know if it's the place or the fact that I can no longer see strands of my hair. I don't know if there's any part of me not transparent.

Note to self: don't come back to the Hereafter unless I'm dead.

Hatter jerks off his hat and violently throws it on the ground at our feet. As I watch, the portal opens again, seeming to spin from inside the hat itself. I'll ask him about that later, and how he got the guests through without his hat. Maybe it's just a tool more than the portal itself, a way to focus his power? He wastes no time before he jumps into the portal, dragging me behind him. I expect to walk through like the last time, stepping into Wonderland the same way I walk through a doorway. Instead, as soon as our bodies cross completely into the portal, we begin to fall. It's the exact same feeling I had when White brought me into Wonderland, like I'm falling down the Rabbit hole all over again. After everything, I'll probably avoid portals for the rest of my life. They definitely aren't on my list of favorite things to do.

There's a strong tug on the arm still wrapped with the Hatter's before I feel him wrenched away from me. I scramble to grasp his hand again, swinging my arm around wildly, but I only swipe through empty air. I scream, terror ripping through me. I can't do this without him. What happens if I don't get where I'm supposed to?

Before I even have time for my voice to crack or grow hoarse, the bright colors of the portal disappear, and then I'm falling for real through open air. I scream again, but I shouldn't have worried. Just when I think I'm going to crack open my skull on the black and white tiles below me, I land in the Hatter's arms with an ungraceful oomph.

"Nice of you to drop in." He grins, his arms strong around me as they cradle my body to his.

I roll my eyes, trying to calm my racing heart, but a small smile curls my lips anyways. He sets me on my feet, and I wobble before I find my balance. I glance down at my arm and smile.

"I'm normal again," I exclaim.

"Well, as normal as normal can be." Hatter chuckles, the grin still on his face. "But what do you consider normal as, to me, you look quite different?"

I laugh at the absurdity of the Mad Hatter telling me I'm not normal. I laugh that I went to the Hereafter, to the literal Afterlife, and I survived. A high fills my body until I feel like jumping up and down and twirling in circles. I'm giddy with joy, happy that the Hatter is here with me and the reason I'm still alive.

In my excitement, I throw my arms around his neck. He stiffens against me, surprise on his face as I smack a noisy kiss on his lips in excitement. The world freezes as I lean back a bit to look into his eyes. His pupils widen slightly before the color darkens from the bright gold of happiness to old gold, glittering like diamonds as he stares into mine. It lasts maybe a second before he growls, the sound animalistic, turning me on in a way I never knew it could.

Before I can respond, the Hatter lifts me by the waist and pushes me back against a wall I didn't even realize was there. His lips slam against mine in a scorching kiss, fire trailing through my body and straight to my core. I let out a squeak of shock before I'm kissing him back just as furiously. I don't hesitate. I guess almost dying really put things into perspective for me. I knew if there was one thing I would regret not doing, it would be not giving into the chemistry between us. So, here I am, sandwiched between a wall and a hard place. Well, a hard something. I've never been so thankful that the Hatter only wears a coat as my hands slide along his defined abs, his muscles tightening beneath my nails as I scrape the rigid lines.

Our teeth clack together in our passion. I have the overwhelming urge to get closer. We're so far apart even though we're so close together. As if he knows what I'm thinking, Hatter's hands drop to my ass and grip tight, hauling me up and against him, my core lining up with the hardness in his pants. I wrap my legs around him, and another growl rumbles in his throat. One hand stays beneath my ass, holding me up, his grip like iron. His other hand slips beneath the hem of my coat, his rough fingers scraping against my skin deliciously. Those fingers slide up my ribs until his thumb barely brushes the underside of my breast. I thread one of my hands into his hair, knocking the top hat from his head. He doesn't seem to care. I tighten my hold to the point of pain as my other dips lower along his abs, towards the waistband of his leather pants.

Someone clears their throat.

Hatter breaks away, a snarl curling his lips, his face more animal than man as he sets me on my feet and twists, hiding me behind him. I'm panting for breath, confused, and so turned on, I might die if I don't get what I want. Uncaring of the threat, apparently, in front of the Hatter, my hands slide around and under his jacket. He was already tense, but when my nails trail along the edge of his pants, his spine cracks as he straightens even more. A breath hisses from his teeth, and his hands still mine against his skin gently. His hand is shaking the tiniest bit, like he's having trouble keeping focused.

"Clara Bee," he sings softly, so only I can hear. "We have company." I don't really care, too deep in my pleasure to ask, but I don't have to. "Meet Tweedledee and Tweedledum."

Chapter 13

Interest and worry cuts through the haze of pleasure flooding my body. I shake my head to clear it, a bit appalled with how easy it was for me to lose myself in the Hatter. It just isn't like me. I guess I'm not really complaining, though.

In all the stories back home, Tweedledee and Tweedledum are short, chubby little men. When I peek around the Hatter's tense shoulders, I stiffen, my fingers clenching in his jacket. There is only one similarity to the stories. They're twins. That I can easily see. Besides that, there's nothing cute or happy about them.

"Dee is on the right. Dum is on the left," Hatter whispers to me, and I look closer.

Dee is definitely a woman, beautiful like a serpent. I have the intense feeling that I'm the prey in this room, and I'm suddenly very relieved for all the weapons strapped to my body. Dee is wearing a skin-tight dress, a dark gold in color. The skirt falls in soft waves from her hips, flaring around her the way models pay someone to arrange. I suspect it has everything to do with the way she moves. Her chest is completely covered in shimmering armor scales, falling across her shoulders and draping down to her navel. The skirt glitters, as if it's covered in crystals that catch the light. The crystals seem to move. When I look closer, I realize they aren't crystals at all. Small metallic beetles crawl across the material, clinging to the fabric.

That isn't even the creepiest thing about Dee. No, her face is the real kicker. From her nose to her neck, she has the most beautiful face I have ever seen. Lips every man wants wrapped around him, a graceful chin and jaw, she's heavenly. But she has no eyes. On her head, great sweeping horns rise high, magnificent dark horns. They curl around her head before coming together in the middle, raising to form sharp points at the top. A few more sharp points stick from the side where the horns are thicker. The base of the horns come down over her forehead, covering where her eyes should be, forming a sort of shield. Something drips down the horns. I don't have the courage to look too closely at it. Dark wavy hair falls down past her shoulders, moving in a nonexistent breeze.

Dum is very much a man, his face as haunting as his sister's. He has eyes, beautiful ice-blue eyes I can see from where I stand. He has a strong jaw, a sharp nose, sharp cheekbones. He also has matching curling horns sprouting from the side of his head, where his ears should be. His are still thick but the curves are more angular whereas his sister's are more smooth. Again, the horns drip something, something red.

Where Dee is all glittering gold, Dum is shades of metallic peacock blue. Armor scales cover him the same way Dee's does, protecting his chest and broad shoulders. The scales stop at his hip where it turns into a long skirt. Long strands of something seem to connect Tweedledee and Tweedledum below the waists, almost like spun thread tying them together. It creates this illusion of a web that the beetles use to climb back and forth between them. Dum's skirt is covered in the insects, as well. I fight the shiver that passes through my body as the twins focus on us. They're beautiful and terrifying all wrapped up together. I tighten my hold on the Hatter.

"Is that who I think it is?" Dum asks, his voice echoing with agony long forgotten.

"It isn't who you think it's not," Dee replies. They both tilt their head to the side at the exact same time. I would have noped right out of here if it wasn't for the Hatter.

"What is it that you see, Tweedledum and Tweedledee?" Hatter's voice is dripping with menace. I'm glad he never uses that voice with me.

"We don't know if it is." Dee.

"But it definitely isn't." Dum.

"It must be Clara Bee," Dee finishes. Jesus. This is too much. Goosebumps rise along my arms. The hairs on the back of my clammy neck stand on end.

The Hatter rolls his shoulders but doesn't respond. I slip my hand into his, finding my courage, before coming to stand at his side, my back ramrod straight. I'm not prepared when their full attention turns to me at the same time. My heart skips a beat, but it helps prevent me from running. My flight sensors are going haywire, though.

"Are you friend?" I ask, my voice surprisingly strong. "Or foe?"

The Hatter growls softly, his hand tightening in mine, but he doesn't say a word, letting me speak.

"Would you see us as a friend?" Dum.

"If you thought we were a foe?" Dee.

"If you're only a foe, then you're no friend," I reply. "If you're a friend, then you're not a foe." My voice is unwavering as I meet them head on.

"What if we are both?"

"What if we are neither?"

"Then you have an opportunity." My voice takes on the same tone I use in the courtroom.

They tilt their heads to the side.

"Do you wish to make a deal, Clara Bee?" they ask together, their voices at once the same, neither masculine nor feminine.

"What does a deal entail?"

The Hatter is growing agitated, shifting from foot to foot. He's obviously nervous about the turn of the conversation, but he doesn't stop me. When I glance at him from the side of my eye, I can't help the sweet feeling that spreads through my body. The Hatter doesn't seem to trust anyone, not even himself. And here he is, trusting me.

"We can make a deal," Dee says.

"For a price," Dum adds.

"Always a price," Dee finishes.

The way they talk puts me on edge, but I'm growing used to it, paying attention to the little nuances between them. Dee seems to be blind, obvious from her lack of eyes. I'm pretty sure Dum is deaf, judging from the horns growing where his ears are supposed to be. But there's no way you can tell it from the way they talk. It's more apparent by the fact that they are holding hands, and when I speak, Dee seems to squeeze Dum's hand. She is his ears, he is her eyes. It works with the freaky twin thing they have going on.

I turn to the Hatter.

"What are the ramifications of making a deal with them?" I ask.

"You must word your wish just right, or else they'll rob you of your sight. Think wisely, then think again, because Dee and Dum are not your friend," the Hatter sings softly, his shoulders quaking with suppressed tension. His eyes don't leave Tweedledee and Tweedledum, keeping them in his sights.

"So, they like to twist the fine print, huh." I smile. "Good thing that's what I do for a living." I turn back towards the twins who are waiting patiently, the only movement from the beetles. "What would your price be to ensure you are our allies?"

Neither speaks. They tilt their heads together like they're having a conversation, their horns missing each other in a way that tells me they are completely in tune. Who knows, they probably have telepathic powers or something. Finally, they lift their heads, focusing on us again.

"A friend ally?"

"Or a foe ally?"

"Both," I reply. "I need both a friend and a foe fighting by my side. I need someone who can think like both."

They tilt their heads together again.

"What are you doing, Clara Bee?" the Hatter whispers. "This won't end well."

"I'm here for a reason, aren't I?" I answer, just as softly, my face serious.

"To overthrow the Red Queen, The Alice."

"Exactly." I squeeze his hand in reassurance. "And I can't do that alone. We need allies."

His chest puffs up, his eyes sparkling as he meets mine. "You have me."

"Do I?" I ask seriously. "When the time comes, you'll stand by my side?"

His face softens, a small smile curling the corner of his lips. He lifts my hand up and kisses the back of it.

"The Mad Hatter and Clara Bee have always been meant to be," he sings, a sweet note in his voice. Then he looks back towards the twins who are waiting patiently for our conversation to finish. I realize we hadn't been watching them that time, and it freaks me out.

"What is your price?" I wait for their answer with bated breath, expecting some sort of treasure or magical item, or my first born child.

"Sight," Dee says.

"Sound," Dum adds.

I wrinkle my eyebrows, glancing at the Hatter.

"Can we do that?" I ask.

He nods his head once. "As long as we succeed."

"Very well," I announce. "In exchange for sight and sound given after we prevail, you will stand at our sides against the Red Queen, before, during, and in the aftermath of the Battle. You will remain loyal to our good cause and be involved." I look at the Hatter. "And you will not harm anyone we consider friend. You will provide council when needed. I will strike this bargain. Do we have a deal?"

They tilt their heads together again, but this time it's a much quicker pause before they speak.

"So, it is now," Dee says.

"So, it shall be," Dum finishes.

A ripple climbs through my body at the finality in the deal. When my wrist begins to burn, I glance down at it in alarm to see a symbol appearing like a brand in my skin. It's a circle with two lines through it in the same shape as the twins' horns. My skin sizzles where it appears, and I grimace at the pain.

The Hatter stares at it, anger flashing in his eyes, but I know it's not directed at me.

"And so, it begins," he snarls. "Down with the reign of the Red Queen."

Chapter 14

The trek back to the Hatter's is interesting. Dee and Dum float silently behind us. They make absolutely no sound, not even the swish of fabric. I have half a mind to ask if they're ghosts after I turn for the fifteenth time to find them much closer than I expect them to be. I'm pretty sure they know they're making me uncomfortable, and I think it amuses them to some extent. If they're capable of feeling emotion that is. The more I think about them, the less I actually know.

I feel weird with them at my back. I know they're predators and turning your back on a predator never ends well. But we had made a deal sealed by the mark on my wrist. I know they can't hurt me while it remains in place, or so the Hatter says. After the battle, and after they receive their payment, they will be even more dangerous. I'll have to make sure to watch my back.

After a long journey through the woods, quicker than the first time since I'm wearing normal shoes, the Hatter's house finally comes into view. Thankfully, I don't have any more run-ins with the Beezles. In fact, all the creatures of Wonderland stay clear of the Tweedles. I can't blame them. It it wasn't for our deal, I would have left them far behind.

I breathe a sigh of relief at the house only to remember that the Knave is the reason that we left in the first place.

"Do we need to worry about the Knave?" I look at Hatter with worry. I don't really want to meet him again for a little while.

"He's gone."

"How do you know?"

Hatter looks at me, his face half serious, half smiling.

"My house is my house, and I can feel every soul."

I raise my eyebrows but ultimately shrug. That isn't the weirdest thing I've heard in Wonderland. Not by a long shot.

Before we can push through the front door, Dormouse opens it from the inside, his face as serious as ever.

"You're late." His voice is bothered, but that's all the emotion I can glean from it.

"For what?" I ask.

"Tea."

I sigh and surprisingly, the Hatter does, too. I was really looking forward to a nice long soak in the tub. Looks like I'll have to put that on hold again.

"The Knave left hours ago. He stuck around for a few minutes but stormed off when you didn't immediately return," Dormouse informs us as we all make our way towards the ballroom. "He was a right prick about it, too."

I'm surprised the Knave didn't just stick around, but when we open the doors, and I see how many guests there are, I realize he had left for a reason, to punish us. There are a total of ten members sitting for tea, and I gasp at the number. Hatter seems equally anguished as we make our way down the table towards our seats. He nods at them all and calls them by name as we pass. The guests nod reverently to him before their eyes flick to me. Every single one of them looks happy to see me, and it makes my heart hurt. I hadn't been able to help them. I need to move faster. I can't shake the feeling that something much worse is coming, and that I need to be prepared.

We take our seats, Hatter in his usual spot and me beside him. The Tweedles take a seat further away, their eyes watching the guests around them. A few of the guests eye them warily, but no one comments as the Tweedles begin pouring themselves tea.

The table, this time, is piled high with food, and I eye it suspiciously. I'm starving, but I don't know if it's worth the risk of getting buzzed. Hatter smiles at my hesitation as he pours us tea.

"It's normal food." He drops the tea pot with a clatter and threads his hands together, placing them under his chin as he watches me. The move gives him a more innocent look that doesn't quite work because I've spent enough time with him. I can see the mischievous glint in his eyes and the tick in his jaw, a telltale sign that he's anything but.

"Normal like me, or normal like you?" I ask. I'm not taking a bite until I know for certain it won't inebriate me.

"Like you."

I lift one of the croissants and take a test nibble. When I don't feel the answering fuzzy sensation, I gobble it down quickly, my starvation taking precedence over manners. Hatter frowns.

"Remind me to make sure you have food more often. I forget that you need nourishment." I hear the shame in his voice at forgetting I might be hungry. I smile at his comment as I wolf down another croissant.

"It's okay. We've been a little busy."

I notice our chairs are dragged closer together now than they usually are, so that our knees brush against each other beneath the table. I fight the urge to slide my hand up his leg and into his lap. It probably isn't appropriate for tea time.

"So," I begin after polishing off three more sweets from my plate. My stomach gives a satisfied gurgle as I sit back in my chair. "Tell me everything."

He pours us both more tea when the cups are empty. This time, my tea is a pastel pink color, and it tastes like blueberries. It's sweet but not overpowering.

"I can show you better than I can tell you," he teases, his voice dripping with sin and sex.

I clench my thighs underneath the table but roll my eyes at him.

"You know what I mean." I take a sip of the tea, humming low in my throat at the taste. My eyes catch on the Hatter's bare chest before dropping down to his lap. When I realize what I just did, I jerk my eyes back up to see the laughter on his face.

"Are you sure you know what you're talking about?" he asks. He leans forward, those old gold eyes making an appearance right before our cheeks touch. "I can show you how mad I can be. All of Wonderland would hear you scream my name," he whispers in my ear.

My body heats up at his words and travels all the way up to my face, which I'm sure flames in response. There's a raging inferno inside of me, and I want to let it out. But now isn't the time even if the tension is so thick between us, I could cry. So, when he pulls back to look into my eyes, I kiss him on the tip of the nose. Surprise makes his lips part slightly and his eyes widen. I smile at the cuteness of it before I lean away and begin to take bites of the food still on my plate.

"I need to know about the Red Queen and how Alice became her." I'm really flying in the dark here. I need more information, so I know what I'm up against.

Hatter smiles softly at me as he settles back in his own seat.

"I can show you that as well." He stands and reaches for my hand. I slip it without hesitation into his. "I will return," he tells the tea party guests as he pulls me behind him. I manage to swipe another croissant before he drags me away completely. Tweedledum and Tweedledee ignore us. They're still sipping their tea, a black mixture I haven't seen before, watching the guests with interest. There's a hunger in Dum's eyes, and it makes me nervous.

"They're all friends," I tell them before we leave the room. I swear I see disappointment on their faces.

Hatter leads me towards the front door and opens it.

"Where are we going?" I ask.

"To see an old friend."

Hatter drags me around the house and into the trees. I say drag because the Hatter takes such long strides that I have to practically jog to keep up. I feel my body grow slick with sweat at the extra work, and I groan. How many times must I boil in this outfit before I get to take a bath?

Once inside the tree line, Hatter slows down enough that I'm able to walk comfortably beside him. We move in silence for about twenty minutes before a small, abandoned cabin comes into view. I squint at it, expecting it to be an illusion the same way the hatter's house is, but it doesn't change. It's tiny, rotting wood and moss covering every inch. Nature has reclaimed it, thick vines climbing the sides and hiding a lot from view. As I stare at the ramshackle house, giggling fills the air, coming from inside. I tense when a man steps through the doorway, the laughter coming from his mouth.

The suit he's wearing used to be luxurious and beautiful. That much I can tell. Now it hangs from him in tatters, moth eaten and dirty. He has two large, brown rabbit ears on his head, but one of them is missing half. They're rough, like they've been chewed on, fur missing in patches here and there. The ear that is more intact is covered in piercings, little jewels flashing at us. I look at his face and realize his entire body mimics his ears. His skin in places is missing or rotting; I can see muscle and bone that I'm not meant to see. He looks like the zombies from TV, just add the bunny ears. I hesitate when the Hatter begins to walk towards the man.

"Hatter," the man exclaims, a gruesome smile full of sharp, bloody teeth spreading across his face.

"March," the Hatter replies, smiling warmly. "I'd like you to meet Clara Bee."

The man, March, gasps loudly, his gaze jerking towards me. It's the first time I notice his eyes are blood red, no pupils to be seen.

"It has begun?" His eyes are wide. I'm not sure if it's fear or wonder in them. The Hatter nods. "Then come, come inside. Come inside. Hurry." March gestures wildly at the door, retreating into the cabin, himself. It creaks as he moves across the floorboards, and I have to wonder how he doesn't fall through the rotting wood.

"The March Hare?" I ask Hatter as we make our way up the steps. They bow under us but don't break.

"Yes."

"What happened to him?" I don't even know how March is still alive with the way he looks.

The smell of mildew makes my nose wrinkle as we climb onto the porch.

"The Red Queen," the Hatter replies.

Then we step inside the cabin, together.

When we step inside the house and my eyes find March again, I can't suppress a gasp. He doesn't look in any way like he did outside. His suit is pristine, his skin smooth. I see no muscle or bone, no mottled flesh. The only flaw on his body is the missing half ear. That's still the same even if his ears are covered in fur and healthy looking. Besides that, he's handsome, strikingly so, even though one of his eyes twitch constantly, drawing my attention every time. It seems more of a tic than an anything. I notice some of his fingers do the same thing, flicking every so often to a rhythm I can't hear.

The house is the same as March. Outside, it looks ready to collapse, barely livable if at all. Inside, it's normal and bright, no mildew smell or rotting wood. It's cluttered but not dirty, warm and inviting.

March giggles when he notices me staring at his ear. I'm trying to figure out why it's the only thing that isn't whole, why everything else is fixed beside the missing chunk.

"It's because it was gone before the red Queen got to me," he says, pointing to the half ear. He accompanies the words with manic laughter, like it's the most hilarious thing he's ever heard. "I got that in a fight with a Bandersnatch. Well, with a different Bandersnatch."

I raise my eyebrows at him but don't comment. I'm not sure if I want to know any more about the Bandersnatch, not after hearing the roar when I was with White.

"Clara Bee wants to learn the history of the Red Queen." Hatter's voice is gentle as March offers us seats at a table. There are books stacked up under one of the legs, keeping it level.

"Of course, of course," he replies, bustling around the kitchen. "Best get to it before the Bandersnatch head this way." He looks at the terror that crosses my face. He giggles, trying to stifle it by putting his hand over his mouth. It doesn't work. "The beasts like to hang around," he offers, "Because the Red Queen set them on me."

"Is that what happened to you?" I think of how he looked outside, like something had tore into him.

His face darkens, the smile dropping instantly. I open my mouth to apologize for asking, but he beats me to it.

"You'll see soon enough." His voice is rough as he grabs jars from the cabinets. He fills a kettle with water and sets it on a stove. He pours a bit from each jar into a tea cup and mixes them together. When the kettle whistles, he pours the boiling water over the ingredients, and a small cloud puffs up in the shape of a heart. He brings the cup to the table and sits it in front of me. I look at the liquid, noting the blood-red color of it.

"Is it safe?" I ask Hatter, staring at the opalescent liquid. White had warned me never to drink tea from anyone, and yet here I am, accepting more tea. I'm terrible with Wonderland rules, apparently. I haven't followed many of them.

He nods before pulling me from my chair and into his lap.

"Take a deep breath, Clara Bee." His arms are strong around me. "It's going to be a rough and intense ride."

With shaking hands, I lift the tea cup and sniff. Roses. It smells like roses and a metallic tang that reminds me of blood. I take a sip of the liquid. At first, nothing happens.

"Did it work?" I ask.

Then the world explodes.

KENDRA MORENO

Chapter 15

I'm flying, or floating. However you want to look at it, my feet aren't touching the ground. I have no idea where I am for a moment, only knowing I feel like I did in the Hereafter. I feel light. I look down in panic and see that I'm whole, but the feeling is still there. I'm floating about a foot from the white and black checkered ground, hovering. I glance around me and realize I'm in the same spot I landed when I came down the Rabbit hole. The table with the Drink Me teacup and Eat Me candy is sitting in the middle of the room. It's the exact same as when I arrived, minus the human skin tablecloth.

A childish scream fills the air when a little girl falls from a portal that opens in the ceiling. She lands hard on her tailbone. I grimace, knowing the pain. As she sits up, terror in her eyes, I make the connection. Blonde hair, blue eyes, and blue and white dress, I'm looking at the original Alice. This must be the first time she fell into Wonderland.

"Hello?" little Alice calls, her eyes looking right past me.

"Can you see me?" She doesn't respond to my question, so I guess there's my answer.

She walks over to the table and stares at the key, curiosity filling her gaze. She picks it up, storing it in a pocket before taking a sip of the tea cup. She shrinks before my eyes and slips through the smallest door. The key opens it.

The world swirls suddenly, and I'm no longer in the Rabbit Hole. I'm sitting at the Mad Hatter's tea table, a guest that no one can see.

Alice is sitting at the table along with Dormouse and March. Dormouse and March giggle and toss food back and forth. My eyes find the hatter and stick to him. He looks so happy and carefree, even if there's still a touch of madness there. He's absolutely beautiful as he smiles at little Alice, his gaze open. I lean closer to him as they all laugh and trade jokes. Even emotionless Dormouse joins in, his face smiling and kind. March tosses a teacup in the air before throwing something at it. The porcelain shatters across the table. Alice laughs and claps her hands with glee.

"Alice," the Hatter laughs as he tosses another teacup in the air. Alice shoots it with a sling shot, exploding more shards onto the setting. They all clap and cheer.

I'm reaching out to touch the Hatter when the scene changes again.

I'm outside a castle in a beautiful garden, one I've never been to before, but it's bright. The castle glitters like a jewel under the sun. I watch as Alice runs giggling from the hedges, a blond boy chasing after her. Their laughter is innocent and filled with friendship. There's three other people in the garden, all with crowns sitting on their heads. One woman is dressed completely in white, her crown studded with white diamonds. Her skin is pale, her hair even paler. Her eyes seem to lack color. She's watching Alice warily. The other two people watch the two children play with smiles on their faces. A man and a woman. I immediately connect them as being the original King and Queen of Wonderland.

"What do we know of this child?" the White Queen asks, a frown upon her face.

"She's just a girl." The King waves away her concern. "Alexander seems to like her. Let them play."

"I don't like it." The White Queen worries her bottom lip as she twists her hands together.

"Calm sister," the Queen ushers. "Everything is fine. She's just a fanciful young girl. What harm can she do?"

The children giggle again from somewhere in the hedges, and I move towards the sound.

"I'm going to find you, Alexander," Alice's young voice calls. The boy giggles from somewhere else in the hedge maze, hiding from her. They must be playing hide and seek. Alice doesn't seem too concerned with finding him, strolling along the hedges, her fingers trailing in the leaves.

A chipmunk scampers from the bushes at the disturbance, and Alice stops, falling to her knees before the creature.

"Come here," Alice whispers to it, holding out her hand. "Come on." The chipmunk takes a few hesitant steps towards Alice, sniffing her fingers. "That's it, little chipmunk."

The little thing climbs into her hand, and she squeezes her fist, trapping it. The chipmunk squeals, and I flinch at the sound, taking a step back. Screams of terror are coming from her fists now, where the chipmunk fights to free itself, scratching and biting at her palms, but she doesn't release the poor thing. Instead, she grips him in both hands and twists, a sickening crunch making my stomach roll. I force myself to watch as blood wells from between her fingers. She grabs an empty pot and catches the bright red liquid inside. When the flow slows, she tosses the lifeless body of the chipmunk into the hedges and runs from the maze.

"Your majesty," she calls, smiling. "I found some paint. Can I paint some of the roses red?"

The Queen giggles.

"Such an imaginative young girl," she coos. "Go ahead, dear."

The White Queen stares at the blood before her eyes flick up and look right at me. I stumble backwards.

The colors swirl.

I'm back at the Rabbit Hole again, staring at the white and black checkered floor. Everything has a darker feel to it, like night has fallen inside. When Alice falls through the portal this time, she doesn't scream. She lands on the floor in a crouch, the tiles cracking beneath her. When she looks up, I freeze. Her hair is still blonde as corn silk. Her dress is still blue and white. But this time, it's covered in blood. So much blood is streaked across the dress, her face, her arms. She's much older, in her thirties maybe, close to my age. She stands and stomps towards the table, scattering everything to the floor. The teacup shatters, spraying the liquid across the tile. White runs from behind a curtain, his clock ticking away. There's fear in his eyes as he runs.

"Fuck!" I hear him mumble as he rushes past me. He's moving so fast, I barely see him transform into a white rabbit and disappear through a door.

"Come back here, White!" Alice screams in rage, storming after him. There's a large bloody knife in her hand.

Colors spin, and I'm staring at the Hatter's house as he steps onto the porch. Worry wrinkles his face as he stares at Alice. She stands in front of him in the grass, watching. White is leaning against the railing, his ears twitching nervously. Cheshire sneers at Alice, his tail swishing back and forth in agitation.

"What happened to you, Alice?" the Hatter asks, his eyes glancing at the blood drip, drip, dripping from the knife. It's fresher than the last time I saw it.

"I grew up," she snarls, taking a step forward. There's only ten feet between them. "When you abandoned me to the woes of reality."

"You've lost your muchness." Hatter frowns at her. Cheshire tenses from his position, his claws sliding out from the tips of his fingers.

"No," Alice replies, stalking right up to him. He doesn't move away. "I've gained power."

She thrusts the knife into the Hatter's heart. Shock clouds his eyes as I scream. Cheshire and White jump into action. I run forward, but the scene changes before I can reach him. I blink at the moisture in my eyes.

I'm in a throne room. Alice sits on an opulent golden chair in a bright-red dress. She wears the same crown on her head the Queen used to wear. Blood runs down her face and neck, pooling against the fabric and darkening it. Bodies litter the floor around the throne, left where they fell. When I look closer, I see the corpses of the King and Queen, their bodies mutilated, their heads cut off and sitting on the steps as a sort of gruesome masterpiece. Their mouths are open in horror. Blood pools beneath them.

Alice holds a heart in her hand, still warm I suspect from when she pulled it from the Queen's chest. I watch from my spot in front of the throne. Alexander stands before her, the bodies of his parents at his feet. He's beaten and bloody, holding an arm at an odd angle. He's older now, too, and the time difference confuses me. He looks like he's closer to twenty one. He watches as Alice brings the heart to her mouth and licks the blood dripping from it. Alexander flinches.

"Alice." His voice shakes. "You're not my Alice."

Quicker than I can follow, Alice is out of the chair and standing in front of Alexander, her hand around his throat. He claws at her hand, gasping for breath as she brings him close.

"I'm not Alice anymore," she snarls in his face. Her other hand leaves a bloody print on his jaw as she cups his cheek. "I'm the Red Queen."

She drags her claws across his face, tearing one side away. He screams in agony, his body going limp from the pain. Blood oozes from the wound before tiny roses spring up in its place. Alexander doesn't fight as she kisses his lips.

My heart beats hard in my chest as the scene changes. I'm afraid of what I'll see next, of how bad this is going to get. I'm standing on a branch in a tree, looking down into a clearing. March sprints past, right into the center. Alice follows on the back of a fearsome creature. It opens its mouth, lips peeling back over its face to reveal sharp, blood-crusted teeth. I realize immediately it must be a Bandersnatch. It can't be anything else. Alice rides on it's back like a horse, glee on her face as they zero in on March. He's stopped in the middle of the clearing, surrounded by more of the creatures. March makes one last effort to get out, sprinting right towards a Bandersnatch. He fakes to the left before moving right, but the beast expects it. My heart stops as the thing tears into March. Blood and pieces fly about the clearing as the other Bandersnatch join in a howl of victory. Tears roll over my cheeks when the screams reach me.

I don't know how much more of this I can take, but I don't have a choice. Whatever drug-induced vision I'm in, I'm stuck until it's over. The scene is changing again, and I pray that this is the last time I'll have to watch something so horrible. Please don't be the Hatter, I think. Please not the Hatter.

I'm standing in a dungeon, the air cold and damp. I shiver even though I'm not really here. Dungeons mean bad things. They always do.

Against the wall, two people are manacled to the stone. Alice stands before them. She's wearing an intricate formal gown, red and glittering with rubies. A high collar frames her dainty neck. The red crown sits on her perfectly teased hair. I move to the side, a small whimper escaping me when I see who is chained to the wall. The White Queen's dress is covered in blood and dirt, but her face is serene even as her eyes glitter daggers. Beside her, the Hatter is chained. He's missing his coat and his hat, but it's him all the same. He's bruised and bloody, like he put up a fight. His pants are unbuttoned and pushed down at an angle, barely hiding his privates. There's blood smeared across his skin. I cry at the implication behind it.

Alice grins wickedly at him.

"You were my friend," the Hatter rasps, his voice full of pain.

"A friend wouldn't have left me to rot in an asylum," Alice hisses back.

She steps towards the White Queen, sharp teeth I have never seen before poking from her lips. The White Queen meets her stare head on, her chin held high.

"No begging your Queen for mercy?" Alice asks her, wickedness dripping from every word.

"You're not *my* Queen." The White Queen's voice is strong when she speaks. Alice yanks the woman's head to the side and strikes, her teeth sinking into the flesh of her neck. A garbled sound passes the White Queen's lips. I watch as she shrivels before my eyes, her skin revealing the bones beneath. Her body sags, her eyes sinking into her skull. Her hair falls to the ground in clumps, only a few strands hanging on. Her crown doesn't fall from her head.

Hatter screams, and Alice yanks away from the body of the White Queen. I watch the Queen's chest rattle, barely rising. She's still alive. Blood drips down Alice's chin, her fangs even longer then before, and she fixes her eyes on the Hatter. I move in front of him, trying to protect him, a pointless act really. She strikes, her hand passing right through me and into the Hatter's chest.

I scream and scream.

I come to, gasping, my heart beating frantically inside my rib cage. I realize quickly my skin is clammy from a cold sweat, the beads still dripping down my forehead. I'm sprawled across the Hatter's lap, his arms wrapped around me, at once strong and gentle.

"Shh," he whispers, pushing strands of hair from my face. I'm sure I look a mess right now. I certainly feel like a mess. "It'll pass. It'll pass."

His voice anchors me to the present, focusing my mind until I no longer hear the Chipmunk's shrieks, the pleas of the Prince, or the hoarse screams of the Hatter.

March sits at the table across from us, sipping tea daintily from a chipped tea cup. Every now and then, he lets out a tiny giggle as he watches us. I haven't decided yet if he's insane or completely broken. I'm betting heavily on the later.

When my heart rate returns to normal, and I no longer feel like I'm going to puke, I sit up in the Hatter's lap. He steadies me as the shakes wrack my body, but otherwise, he lets me adjust at my own pace.

"What the hell was in that tea?" I ask March. My voice is still rough, either from screaming or the tea, I'm not sure.

He grins, a giggle escaping his throat. The ears on his head twitch back and forth, like they don't really know which way to point anymore.

KENDRA MORENO

"Reali-Tea," he whispers before clamping his hands over his mouth to stop a full laugh. He's not successful. He ends up spitting all over the table as a deep-bellied hysteria overtakes him. He falls from the chair, roaring his amusement while he rolls on the floor. I stare at him, one eyebrow raised. I glance at the Hatter's face. He wears the same amusement, like he wants to join March in the giggles on the floor, but when his eyes focus on me, he gains control over the impulse.

"How are you here?" I ask softly, turning on his lap to face him straight on.

"I am neither here nor there," he replies. "I am everywhere."

I grasp the sides of his face seriously, urging him to focus on me alone. March's laughter fades into background noise as I stare deeply into his eyes.

"I saw you die." My voice cracks on the last word. "I saw you die twice."

He studies me intently.

"As long as Wonderland lives, so, too, do I. Remember, Clara Bee?"

"But you can feel pain?" I clarify because those images will stick with me for the rest of my life. I will have nightmares of those screams, of seeing the Hatter die again and again.

He nods his head, his cheeks warm beneath my palms. I feel the tears spring to my eyes unwillingly, the realization that he must have felt such terrible agony, that if I can't fulfill my part in the prophecy, he could feel it again, too much. I've been in this world a matter of a few days— at least, I think it's been a few days— but I already feel like I belong. I don't want to fail them all. A single tear tracks down my face, and he stares at it in wonder.

"Don't cry for me, Clara Bee," he whispers softly. "I don't think I can bear it."

"I'm sorry." I lift my hand to wipe away the tear, embarrassed that I'm losing it.

He catches my hand in his own before I manage the task. His eyes are filled with emotion as he leans forward and kisses the droplet away, his lips soft against my skin. It's enough to choke me up again, but I fight against it. It feels like a losing battle.

"Never be sorry." He looks into my eyes. "Not for me. Our world is in chaos, every one of us suffers in some way. My mind," he taps the side of his head, "is where I suffer. Inside my thoughts, there's chaos, insanity, fear. I cannot fight it. I cannot push it away. But inside all that chaos, there's you, shining bright, my own star to light the way and show me the path home. Never be sorry for who you are," he says, more serious than I have ever seen him. "Because who you are is everything to me."

I melt. Right there in his lap in the insane March Hare's rotting cabin, March still rolling on the floor, wheezing, fighting for breath. If I'm being honest with myself, it's the moment I fall in love with the Mad Hatter, so crazy and tortured that he sings in riddles and rhymes and yet, he can spin such beautiful words that ring of truth and love. We might be prophesied to be together, but a prophecy didn't make me love the Hatter. The man in a coat and a top hat did that all on his own.

On the floor, March suddenly sits up, his ears standing straight and pointing in the same direction for once.

"Shh, do you hear that? Do you hear it?" he whispers. His nose twitches.

We pause, listening. Everything is silent. And then a loud screech fills the air, the noise jarring and loud. I feel like ice picks are thrust into my ears even though the Hatter clamps his hands over them. I watch blood trickle from his ear canals when they remain unprotected. I clamp mine around his in an attempt to help. The screeching stops, but whatever it is, it's very close.

"Bandersnatch." March's voice quivers. "It's the Bandersnatch."

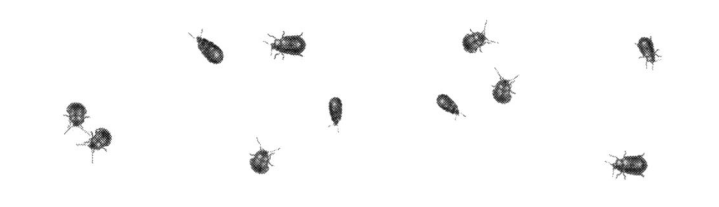

Chapter 16

"Go! Go! You must go!" March yells. He giggles and then begins to sing the same words over and over again, dancing around in circles. It's exactly the thing that makes my anxiety crank up a notch. Nothing like a raving lunatic twirling around and singing your doom when death is waiting right outside the door.

I assume the Bandersnatch are the same beasts I saw the Red Queen riding on in the tea-induced vision. No one has specifically told me what they look like, but that sound they make, it's the same as the one I hear now. If it really is the same creatures, we need to move fast. I don't have any desire to meet the beasts head on.

The Hatter doesn't waste any time at all before he's grabbing my hand and pulling me towards the back of the cabin.

"You didn't drink your tea!" March shouts, and a teacup shatters against the wall before us, the glass shards raining down. Tea drips down the wall, leaving a red stain behind. It looks just like blood. The Hatter doesn't even react.

The screech sounds again, a little closer than before. The Hatter isn't fast enough to cover my ears this time, and I feel wetness run down the side of my neck. I grimace, grinding my teeth against the pain.

Hatter leads me to a back door I hadn't noticed before. It's designed to look more like the wall, blending in so as to hide it. Hatter shoves it open and tugs me out after him. It's a wonder my arms are still attached. I seem to get dragged around a lot in Wonderland.

I have a moment of panic that we're walking out into the same forest as those creatures, but I don't have time to focus on it. We step into the tree line. We pick up our pace until we're practically sprinting through the trees. I focus, instead, on not tripping over the roots beneath our feet.

Hatter's house isn't far away, only a twenty-minute leisurely walk. I know it isn't far, but it seems so much further when you're running for your life. There is no way we can outrun the Bandersnatch. Even the March Hare couldn't, and he had been fast.

Tree branches rip at the train of my coat behind me, tearing at my already tangled hair. The Hatter tries to keep the worst branches from hitting me in the face as he pulls me, but he can only do so much. I feel the wood making small cuts across my cheeks, but it's the least of my worries right now. I feel my energy wane, the little sleep I've gotten wearing on me.

The Bandersnatch screeches draw closer, growing louder and more frequent, like hounds that have picked up our scent. For the first time, I realize there's more than one, after all. There are too many screeches. I can barely hear past the roaring in my ears and the thumping of my heart, but their calls still pierce through the sounds. My chest squeezes, and I trip, but I never hit the ground. Hatter's grip is like iron, and I'm on my feet again before I even realize I'm falling.

My breath saws in and out, my heart threatening to burst from my chest. My legs stumble through the underbrush, the Hatter the only reason I keep going. I can't breathe. I can't breathe. I can't breathe.

I hear teeth snap behind me, the sound of jaws slamming shut on a snarl.

It's taking too long. We aren't going to make it. The Bandersnatch are closing in.

We are going to die.

"Hatter," I wheeze, terror clawing at my throat. My legs are moving slower, my body beginning to shut down.

He looks back at me. His eyes lift over my shoulder, and they widen in fear. For just a moment, there's absolute terror on his face.

"Hatter," I repeat, and I know he can hear the horror in my voice. The acknowledgment of what is going to happen next. I can't keep going. I'm not strong enough.

His face hardens, and he jerks my arm hard, my shoulder popping from the sudden move of him pulling me into his body. He pauses our stride barely a second to scoop me over his shoulder, his arms locking around my legs to keep me secure. The last bit of air in my lungs whooshes out of me as his muscles dig into my abdomen hard.

"Hang on, Clara Bee," he shouts, and then we're moving faster.

But not fast enough. Nowhere close to enough.

Thrown over his shoulder as I am, I have a prime view of what's behind us, how close they are. I wish I couldn't see them. Three great, hulking creatures bound through the trees, running side by side, dodging trees in their path. They don't seem to mind the branches or the undergrowth. Instead, they seem to break through everything they barrel past, their bodies absorbing the impacts. They are pitch-black in color, resembling giant wolves you see in horror movies back home. These are like no wolves I have ever seen, though.

Much like the March Hare, they're rotting in places. One is missing his great red eye, a gaping hole where it used to be. I can see the bone underneath, glaring white against the black fur. I clamp my hands over my ears when one lets out another screech, lifting his head into the air as if to howl. The sound is deafening this close. They snarl, blood dripping from their maws as they open their mouth wide, the skin folding back over their face to reveal the sharp teeth inside. Their teeth look a mixture between an angler fish and a saber-toothed tiger. But the Bandersnatch aren't the most terrifying things behind us.

Riding on the back of the Bandersnatch in the middle rides a woman. Her skin is pale, her hair such a pale-blonde that it looks more white than yellow. Her dress is blood-red, the same color as the blood dripping down her chin, down her neck, and smeared around her eyes. The dress has a massive skirt that flies behind her as the Bandersnatch bounds forward. On her head, sits a blood-red crown, dripping with jewels. It catches the light from nearby glowing plant life, sending sparkles like fireflies around her. She's wearing the most evil smile I've ever seen. I recognize Alice instantly.

"Hatter!" she roars, her face scrunching into a look of pure rage.

The Hatter runs harder, pushing himself as fast as he can go.

"Hatter," I whisper, choking on the word. My hands clench in his jacket at his back. "We have to go faster."

I can feel him panting beneath me, the run wearing on him. The extra weight he carries, it's slowing him. I'm slowing him down.

"Leave me." My voice wobbles. His arms tighten around my legs, to the point of pain, but I don't comment on it. "Leave me and run."

"Stop it!" he pants. "I won't."

"We're going to die. If you leave me, you'll escape."

"No!" he roars. "I won't allow it!"

I look at the Red Queen again and meet her eyes. She grins, and I remember all the pain she's caused Wonderland, all the pain she's caused the Hatter. I want to hurt her. I want her to pay for her sins, for her crimes. I want to be able to fight her. Realization dawns on me.

"The gun!" I exclaim, smacking the Hatter on the back. "The gun! Please tell me the gun is still in my holster!"

Cheshire had armed me with the Heart Breaker, and Hatter had slipped it back into my holster when we were trying to escape the Knave. Hatter's shoulders tense, and his breath shudders.

"It's in your holster still. You still have it," he wheezes.

I run my hands up the Hatter's back and to my hip, reaching for the holster. My fingers wrap around the grip, and I yank the gun free, the snaps popping open that kept it secure.

The Red Queen is close enough now that I can make out the color of her eyes. Pitch black, no pupils, no whites. She looks like the demon she is.

The riding is rough, but I'm able to hold the large gun in my hands, ready to point it at the bitch on the Bandersnatch. My abs cramp at the strain of lifting my body up enough to aim. I grit my teeth against the pain.

"Wait!" The Hatter's voice is barely more than a rasp at this point, his breath sawing in and out. "A clearing."

Just as he says it, we break through the trees, right into the clearing he mentioned. He stops right in the middle, spins and plants me on my feet at the same time. I raise the gun and point it at the Red Queen entering the clearing on the back of the Bandersnatch. For once, my hands don't shake, my anger giving me strength I didn't know I have. The Hatter stands behind me, his hands on my shoulders, bracing me for the recoil of the gun. I assume it's going to be a strong one. I will probably need all the help I can get.

To the Queen's credit, she doesn't seem bothered at all by the gun I have trained on her. The two Bandersnatch flank her sides, spreading out. There's more snarls behind us, and I feel the Hatter spin, putting his back against mine.

"There's three more behind us," he whispers. I can still hear the whistle in his breath, his body heaving from the exertion.

"What are the chances we make it out of this alive?" I ask, my voice hard.

He doesn't reply, and I take it for the answer it is. I reach behind me with my weaker hand and grip his tight in my own. If I'm going to die, at least, I'm not alone.

"Well, well, well, what do we have here?" the Red Queen, Alice, asks, tilting her head unnaturally to the side. I'm angry that her voice still sounds sweet even though it's dripping with malice.

Neither of us answer her. I stare her down, keeping the gun trained on my target.

"Has the Hatter gained another pet, hmmm?" she asks. "Did he tell you I used to be one of his pets?" I watch her, the gun aimed right at her heart. "Did he tell you how he destroyed me?"

"I see nothing but a woman who is exactly who she is. The Hatter didn't turn you into a monster. You *are* a monster," I growl.

She laughs, the sound like tinkling glass.

"You're a cute one. Pray tell, what is your name, woman?"

I grin at her, bracing against the Mad Hatter's back as I prepare myself. Her eyes narrow.

"I'm Clara Bee," I reply.

I have the satisfaction of seeing her eyes widen in shock before I pull the trigger. A sound like a bomb going off echoes around the clearing, the force of the shot shoving me back hard against the Hatter. We both stumble, but he keeps us from falling, grunting under the force of the recoil. Whatever bullets are inside the chamber, three of them shoot from the barrel. I watch almost in slow motion as the bullets explode outward, sharp points spinning around them as they head for their targets. Apparently, the gun aims itself because two of the bullets go for the flanking Bandersnatch. I watch one snarl, its lips peeling back over its face and razor sharp teeth snapping as it tries to avoid the bullet. It isn't fast enough. The bullet hits dead center, ripping through brain matter and skull and exiting the other side, before finally embedding in a tree. The tree trunk shatters, and it begins to fall backwards, away from the fight.

The other Bandersnatch dodges, but it still hits its chest. Both of the beasts go down, crumbling into furry heaps on the ground. It sends the remaining Bandersnatch into chaos. They snap their teeth, snarl, great globs of saliva dripping from their jaws, but I ignore them all. My eyes are riveted to the last bullet, the one meant for the Red Queen.

Her Bandersnatch isn't quick enough either. It rears up on its hind legs, exposing it's soft underside. The bullet enters its sternum. The other bullets tore through the others with no resistance. It doesn't meet any this time either. The bullet passes right through the beast and slams into the Red Queen's stomach, sending her flying from its back and to the ground in a heap of red material. A scream of rage echoes around the clearing. I don't get a chance to breathe a sigh of relief.

That shot would have killed anyone else. Hell, it would have killed an elephant. The Red Queen immediately springs from the ground, her hand clamped over the wound as she takes a step towards us. Blood wells around her fingers, dripping down the front of her dress.

"You ruined my dress!" she snarls.

I raise my eyebrow at that one. A dress with a hole seems a lot less important than a hole in her body. Maybe she needs to get her priorities straightened out. She stoops, reaching down to the whimpering Bandersnatch dying at her feet. It gives a cry of pain when the Red Queen punches her fist through its chest. Her hand comes back out, blood coating all the way to her elbow, a large heart in her hand. The beast doesn't make another sound. She smiles gleefully at me as she licks the blood dripping from the heart. I watch in horror as the giant hole in her stomach begins to stitch itself back together, right before my eyes.

"What do we do?" I ask Hatter frantically.

The three Bandersnatch behind us are closing in, and the Hatter growls at them, the sound completely animal and terrifying. It doesn't stop their advance at all.

His eyes meet mine, resolve in them as he spins and wraps his arms around me.

"Hell no! We are not giving up now!" I growl, raising the gun again.

I squeeze the trigger three more times, the bullets spreading and spinning as soon as they exit the barrel. The Red Queen grins as she dodges every single one of them, her movements too fast to follow with my eyes. One bullet hits another Bandersnatch, but the other two learned from their brethren and avoid them.

"Clara Bee," the Hatter whispers into my neck, holding me tight. "My Clara Bee."

The last two Bandersnatch spring towards us, and I close my eyes, clenching a fist in the Hatter's jacket. I draw the short sword at my hip, intending to take one down with me even if I don't want to see it. I'm not going down without a fight. I hope it's painless, but I know that's a silly thing to hope for in this circumstance.

A hiss echoes through the clearing, and I crinkle my eyebrows in confusion. When I open my eyes, blue smoke is billowing from a canister in front of us. The Red Queen shrieks in anger as four more clatter onto the ground. The Bandersnatch whimper and back away, afraid of the smoke touching them. I watch in wonder as the blue smoke completely hides us from view. The Hatter laughs with glee, picking me up and spinning me around.

"What's going on?" I ask just as a cloaked figure breaks through the smoke, coming right for us.

Masculine hands reach out and grab both of ours, nearly ripping my arm from its socket again as he yanks us behind him. We go right past the last two Bandersnatch, snapping and snarling. They don't seem to be able to see us, the smoke making them shake their heads in agitation. The sounds fade behind as we sprint through the trees. The stab in my side starts up again. My body is exhausted, but I keep pushing. We have a chance to survive. I won't let my endurance be the reason we don't make it.

"Hurry," the cloaked figure ushers, the voice definitely that of a man's. "We only have a few more minutes before the smoke clears."

We stop abruptly at a large tree, the trunk at least double the size of a redwood. There are chunks carved out of the bark, and when the cloaked man begins to climb, I realize they're hand holds, forming a ladder.

The Hatter lifts me off the ground and places me as high on the trunk as possible, urging me to follow the cloak above me. I don't mention that I'm scared of heights as I begin to climb. It doesn't seem that important at the moment. Just don't look down. Don't look down. I repeat that in my head all the way to the top where the man reaches down and pulls me over the edge. He does the same for the Hatter. We both collapse to the floor, our breaths ragged. I'm sure my heart will never beat the same again.

I look up as the man lowers his hood and do a double take. He's handsome and definitely younger than me. Somewhere in his twenties I guess. His skin is blue, and I can see the tips of pointed ears peeking through long chestnut hair. His mouth is set in a grim line as he crosses his arms over his chest, making the muscles in his biceps bulge. His eyes are a brilliant turquoise. He doesn't speak, and the

Hatter doesn't seem intimidated by him at all. Hatter begins to giggle, covering his eyes. The sounds bounces back and forth between sounding like laughter and sounding like sobs.

The entire inside of the tree looks like a house, all hewn into the wood itself. The walls are rough where they were carved, and there are doorways. The floors are covered with pillows and rugs. The only accessory I can see is some weird material hanging from the ceiling in a corner—it looks like some sort of sack— and a hookah standing in the middle of a pile of pillows.

From a doorway carved in the side, another man steps out. He walks with a cane, hunched over it as he shuffles inside. He's clearly elderly, his skin the same blue as the younger man, though more weathered. His eyes are pure white, nothing inside the orbs. There's no cloudy pupil to indicate blindness. He's wearing nothing but some type of bright-blue loincloth, his chest covered with liver spots and odd symbols I've never seen before. A beard drops from his chin to his knees. It looks like moss, and there are all manner of bugs crawling through it, like he's a living habitat.

Then he smiles, gaping holes where teeth are missing. My skin crawls.

"And who are you?" he rasps.

Chapter 17

I fight the intense urge to take a step back, knowing behind me is a fall that can kill me if I go over. I know the Hatter would prevent me from falling, but I have no desire to even imagine a possibility where he wouldn't. Instead, I hold my ground. Goosebumps run up and down my arms as the old man hobbles into the center of the room, his pace slow and measured. The cane clacks against the wood of the floor, the blow only softening when he shuffles over a rug.

He had asked me a question, but I don't answer. I'm not sure if I want to. The old man's eyes trail around the room, and I realize he could possibly be blind. I'm not sure since there is no pale iris or pupil in the milky depths, but he never focuses on anything too long. I know nothing in Wonderland is what it seems, so I don't accept it as fact just yet. I nod to myself when the old man's eyes stop spinning and fix, completely steady, on the Hatter. Not blind then. Or, at least, maybe not one hundred percent.

"We thank you for your assistance," the Hatter speaks, bowing slightly to the old man. He tips his hat to him for good measure as he threads his fingers through mine. The touch helps to calm me.

"Hatter," the old man replies fondly. His voice is husky, like he's smoked a lot of cigarettes throughout his life. "You've dropped in at a most unfortunate time. It's my purging."

"I apologize. If you have a moment to spare, the prophecy, please, won't you share?" Hatter's fingers twitch in mine. Not for the first time, I wonder if he can't help the rhymes that slip from his lips. Maybe the lyrical habit is a product of his madness.

The old man grins at the Hatter, his eyes moving from him and focusing on me. I tense.

"Wonderland has chosen wisely." His eyes meet mine. I have no idea how I know. There's literally no pupils but nevertheless, I know the exact moment we're looking directly into each other's eyes. "Clara Bee, I presume?"

"Yes." My voice is raspy, and I have to clear my throat and repeat myself to actually be heard.

The old man seems to study me, taking in every detail from my feet to the rat's nest on my head. I'm not sure what he sees. I'm in dire need of a shower. I can't remember the last time I felt clean. I'm wearing the same clothes that I escaped from the Knave in, burned up in the humid Hereafter, faced off with Tweedledee and Tweedledum, sat through a tea party, drank some Reali-Tea, and ran from a pack of Bandersnatch and the Red Queen. To say I stink is an understatement. How I look has to be worse. My hair feels like it's in tangles, knots that probably won't come out with a saw, catching my fingers when I run my hand through them self-consciously. Do I even look human anymore? When was the last time I slept? How long ago had it been since I first landed in Wonderland?

Whatever he sees, he makes a decision and gestures to the younger man standing off to the side. The young man immediately walks over and assists him towards the Hookah sitting in the middle of room. There's pillows all around it. He takes a seat slowly on one side before pointing to the other cushions. The Hatter leads us over, and we sink into our seats. The pillows are incredibly soft, and I instantly feel like laying my head down and taking a nap, the exhaustion catching up with me. I force myself to open my eyes wide and focus on the old man.

"We can talk while I prepare," he says. The young man unhooks the pipe of the hookah and passes it to him. It's that moment that it dawns on me. I know exactly who I'm talking to.

"You're the Blue Caterpillar." My voice is a bit awed as I look at him. Then I look at the younger man. "You have a son?"

The Caterpillar laughs.

"No, Child. He is only an extension of me."

I frown. What the hell does that mean? Should I ask or let that weird bit of information go? I decide to let it go for now. I can always ask the Hatter later.

"What do I call you?" I ask. Everyone else seems to go by only a portion of their name. White. Hatter. March. Is he Blue or Caterpillar?

He shrugs.

"Old. Young. Blue. Caterpillar. Absolem. It makes no difference to me. I am all."

He takes a drag from the hookah, holding the smoke in for a moment before breathing the blue smoke out. It curls out in front of us, forming circles and swirling before shaping into creatures. I watch in fascination as a rabbit forms in the haze. And then it begins to move, hopping around the room, glowing from within as it runs. There's a silhouette forming next, a man with a top hat. I glance at the Hatter. He's enraptured with the show. When I look again, there's another silhouette that looks suspiciously like me. The two silhouettes come together in an intimate embrace before dancing around the room in each other's arms. More shapes move, but I can't focus on them without taking my eyes from the dancing couple. Absolem speaks again.

"Clara, you must have many questions."

Behind us, the young man bustles around the room, moving things and preparing something on the stove. There's a distinct smell of dirt and flower coming from his direction. I have so many questions to ask the man in front of us, puffing away on his hookah, but I hesitate. I have no idea where to begin.

"Come, come, Child. Do not fear me. Ask what you wish to know." He says this around the mouthpiece. He offers it to the Hatter, but he shakes his head. When he offers to to me next, I do the same. If the Hatter doesn't want to do it, I definitely don't.

"Are you psychic?" If I'm correct, then that means the prophecy came from the Blue Caterpillar, and here I am sitting across from him. He should know all the answers.

He chuckles.

"I have been gifted, cursed, to see the past, the future, the present."

"And these things are set in stone?"

"The future is a flowing river. It is not a wall. I see many possibilities. I see many outcomes."

"How do we know which one is correct?" I ask.

"We don't. The future changes as quickly as I see it."

Frustration makes me shift in my seat on the pillows.

"Then how do we even know I'm the one in the prophecy?"

I don't say how much pain it will cause me if the prophecy isn't about me after all. I had already let myself fall for the Hatter. The thought of leaving Wonderland to pave the way for another woman destined to be with the Hatter sends a bolt of agony through my chest. I don't think I could survive the heartbreak.

"In all the possibilities, there is one constant." He pulls on the Hookah again. "The Prophecy. And your name never changes. Wonderland only has one possibility of survival."

"Only one?" That seems horribly bad odds for the future of a world. One in how many other futures? How many chances do we fail?

"Only one."

"But there's no guarantee that we can succeed?"

"Nothing is guaranteed, Child."

I sigh. The Hatter smiles at me in encouragement. It's exactly what I need. I straighten my spine, determination to do my part fueling me.

"What exactly is the prophecy?" I've heard my portion, but I want to know the whole piece. There could be something we're missing.

Absolem smiles around the hookah. The lights in the room dim considerably, and a glow spreads out from him. Small glowing specks appear in the air, dancing around with the shapes forming in the smoke. Everything around us narrows down on Absolem; I no longer hear the young man bustling around the room. Hatter squeezes my hand as he removes his hat, his eyes focused on the smoke and light show in front of us.

When Absolem begins to speak, his voice echoes, power dripping from every word. I suddenly realize the profoundness of what is happening. I'm hearing my possibilities, and the possible fate of Wonderland if we succeed.

"The first of three is Clara Bee
Who will come to set Wonderland free,
She'll tame the Hatter and down the Knave
Because Clara Bee fights for the brave.
A triad begins to destroy the Queen
Though nothing is ever as easy as it seems,
She must lose her heart while taking a stand
To the first son of Wonderland.
The second comes in the dead of night
After saving the life of Wonderland's White,
She'll befriend the creatures of the day
And strip the Red Queen's immortality away.
Destined for the second son of Wonderland,
She'll conquer his heart and take his hand,
The triad will be two strong
And right the things that have been wronged.
To complete the triangle, one must ask
How the third son wears his mask,
He'll fight the hold, but best be quick
Or he'll lose his chance with each tick tock tick.
The third completes the triad of three
Bringing strength and the fall of the Red Queen,
Stronger together as they take their stand
To save the Sons of Wonderland."

As the final words of the prophecy fade away, the glow dims, and the room returns to normal. I let out the breath I had been holding, loosening my grip on the Hatter who I had been squeezing the crap out of. He doesn't seem to care. His focus is on my face, worry on his brow. I smile to let him know I'm okay, and it relaxes him.

"So, there will be three of us? Who are the Sons of Wonderland?" I ask. Obviously, the Hatter is one of them, but I want to confirm who the other two are. I have a good idea, though.

"Yes. Hatter is one. White is another. Cheshire is the last."

I sigh.

"Cheshire doesn't seem the kind to let a prophecy tell him what to do."

"No," Absolem agrees, but he doesn't elaborate, and I drop it for now, focusing on my portion.

"So, my job is to tame the Hatter," I glance at Hatter, but he doesn't seem bothered by the term, "And down the Knave. How do I do that?"

Absolem chuckles, shaking his head in amusement.

"That is up to you, Child. Only you know the answer."

"But you see the future. Can't you tell me how I do it?"

He shakes his head again.

"It doesn't work like that, Clara. I see the possibility. I see the result. I don't always see the journey."

The young man shuffles over to us then, and he lifts Absolem from the cushion. His bones crack and snap as he straightens the best he can, wrapping weathered fingers around the cane. My eyes focus on the beard again, the moss, and the various insects crawling around. I suppose a caterpillar would feel a sort of kinship with other insects.

The young man leads Absolem to the dark sack hanging from the ceiling in the corner of the room. It blends into the carved walls, the outside panels appearing wet when they reflect the light back at us. The young man begins helping him into the chamber. It sways under the movement. The oddity of the situation doesn't even affect me anymore. The smoking Blue Caterpillar climbing into what I suspect is a cocoon? Nothing. Weird bugs in his beard? Understandable. If I ever go back home to my world, I imagine it will seem incredibly boring after all this.

The chamber slowly begins fusing together. Absolem smiles at us, the missing teeth making it eerie.

"But won't you tell me how to save Wonderland?" I try one more time. I need more information. I need to know everything.

The Hatter doesn't speak, his eyes watching the Caterpillar slowly disappears inside the cocoon.

"Follow your heart," he says. "You are Clara Bee the Brave. I must purge. I will see you on the other side." Then his face hardens, and he speaks once more before he's sealed in completely. "Show no mercy, Child. You can't afford to."

When the words register, Absolem is gone, wrapped inside a man-sized cocoon while we stare at it. I have no idea what will come out when he finishes his purging. I'm not sure I want to know. But I have a mission. I look towards the Hatter. He's already looking at me, a small smile on his face. There is a touch of madness in it, but it only endears him to me more. My body sags, and I lounge back on the pillows.

"You need to sleep." Hatter moves around some of the pillows, arranging them into a bed. "Lay down. We can go home after you rest for a while."

"Don't we need to go now?" I yawn around the words, kind of ruining the urgency I want to infuse into my question.

"You won't make it in your condition. I'm tired, too. We'll rest and then go home to clean up."

"Please. I really need a shower and some new clothes." I lay down on the pillows, my body relaxing quickly.

His eyes darken as he grins.

"I will do whatever Clara Bee sees fit to demand of me."

"Then let's go home and down the ladder, so that I can finally enjoy my Hatter," I reply to his delight. "After the nap, of course."

I close my eyes. I figure it will be impossible to sleep in the same room as a giant cocoon where an old man is "purging" whatever it is he needs to. It's weird and creepy, but my body is so damn exhausted, it doesn't seem to have a flight instinct anymore. The Hatter lays down beside me, and I curl into his side. Seconds pass, and I sink into a deep, dreamless sleep.

Chapter 18

There's no sign of the Bandersnatch or the Red Queen when we finally wake and descend the ladder. I feel so refreshed when I rub the sleep from my eyes. The cocoon still hangs in the corner, no movement or noise coming from it. I realize the young man is gone, but I don't ask. Maybe he disappears when Absolem is purging. I don't know. I don't really want to know. I just accept it as a fact of Wonderland. Some things have no explanation.

We don't go far before we're passing through the clearing where we had the standoff, where I had shot the Red Queen with the most insane bullets only for her to stand up and accuse me of ruining her dress. There are no bodies from the four fallen creatures. There isn't even any blood left behind. The clearing is as pristine as if we had never been there. It's unsettling.

"They're part of the Queen," Hatter offers as an explanation. "They live because she wills them to."

"So, what are they exactly? Zombies?"

"No." He looks ahead, his face somber. "And yes. Their bodies are alive, but their souls are dead. Passed to the Hereafter. They're mostly just empty vessels."

"They used to be people?" I ask in horror. It had never crossed my mind that the gruesome creatures could have been anything other than what they are.

He nods but doesn't say anything more. I decide to leave the subject alone for now, seeing the obvious grief it causes. There is so much sadness in wonderland, in a place that always seems so magical on paper. I don't know how the Hatter does it, watching the people he cares about being killed one by one, watching his world be destroyed by someone he once called friend, all while going on living. It's a burden, to not be able to die with those friends, one that certainly has taken its toll. Yet, he still does it, without complaint, without disdain. He still escorts every single soul to the Hereafter and settles them into their life there. The thought humbles me. Helping the downtrodden has always been a passion of mine. The fact that the Hatter and I have that in common is amazing even as it's sad. I wish we didn't have to do the jobs we do, but someone has to do it. And I would rather it be me, or the Hatter, than someone who doesn't care, or isn't affected by it. The man behind the madness is so much more than his insanity. He is so much more than he appears, than he thinks.

"What is it you think, when you look at me like that?" the Hatter asks suddenly. I flush. Had I been looking at him while I was lost in thought?

"Look at you like what?"

"Like I am some wondrous creature. You look at me in wonder," he replies softly.

I thread my fingers through his and smile up at him.

"You *are* wondrous. Is that not okay? If I look at you like that?" His face grows serious, and I frown. "Hatter?"

"Insanity is a disease that eats away at my mind. I am not some magical, beautiful thing," he growls. "I am madness and death, and I do not deserve the look in your eyes. I am a monster that cannot die as a monster should."

Those words are wrong. Utterly wrong. I see the beauty in his madness. I see the man beneath it all, his soul begging for someone to bring him out of the loneliness. His words strike me in the heart, and I can't think of anything to say. I open my mouth. Say something. Say anything. Tell him he's worthy. Tell him he's perfect the way he is. Tell him I want it all, every last bit of it, as long as he'll have me.

"Hatter."

He growls, and I stop at the agony in the sound. Agony I'm responsible for. I wait for him to speak again, but he doesn't, no matter how much I plead with my eyes or tug on his hand. The silence is thick with tension, the walk back to the house is torture. Somewhere along the way, I said something wrong. Or I did something wrong, and it brought out a side of the Hatter I haven't seen before. It's a side I want to hug and hold and tell everything will be alright if he'll let me. I feel the desperation coming from him in waves.

We enter the meadow, his home coming into view in front of us. He drops my hand and speeds up, practically running towards the door.

"Hatter! Wait!" I cry, trying to catch up with him, but I'm no match for his long stride on a good day. As of now, my legs are still weak and feel like jello.

He's slamming the door open just as I climb the porch. Dormouse stands on the other side, his face serene as the Hatter storms past. On his way through, the Hatter picks up a particularly ugly vase displayed on a pedestal and slams it against the wall. It shatters, ceramic pieces flying around the entry way. I watch as blood trickles down his hand, brilliant red against his pale skin. It brings about memories of the visions, of the blood I saw pouring from his chest, and I fight a wave of nausea.

"Oh, Hatter." I move towards him, intending to wipe the blood up no matter how much my stomach roils.

"The Knave returned," Dormouse speaks. "But he left again when you weren't in."

I stop and stare at Dormouse. There's still no emotion on his face, and I have to wonder again if he even has any at all.

"Kill the knave, kill the knave. Off with his head to free the slave," Hatter mumbles in agitation, standing in the middle of the ceramic shards, staring at the blood dripping from his hand onto the floor. He repeats the lines, angrier with every word.

I place my hand on his shoulder in comfort, and he jerks away, hard. He slams his fist into the wall, in the same spot as the vase met its fate. He leaves a bloody mark behind where there is a crater, and when he storms away into the ballroom, there's a trail of blood behind him. I move to follow him.

"I wouldn't," Dormouse says, his monotone voice halting me.

"Why not?"

"When he's under stress, his madness comes out more. There's no telling what he might do."

"He would never hurt me. And besides, this is the time that he needs someone the most," I defend. I don't want to leave him alone. "Is there a tea party going on?"

"No. The next one isn't due until tomorrow. But he still has to pass the last guests. They've been waiting for him."

I worry my bottom lip, staring at the spots of blood on the floor.

"At least, give him a little time to calm down," Dormouse says. "I've set food in your room, and the wardrobe is stocked full of clothing. Perhaps you can make use of the facilities."

"Are you telling me I stink, Dormouse?" I ask, cocking my eyebrow at him.

I swear his lips twitch, but I can't be sure.

"I would never tell the Clara Bee she smells like the rear end of a Jabberwocky," he says.

I snort and shake my head. I mockingly bow to him, exaggerating the movements, before heading towards the stairs instead of the ballroom. Dormouse is right; I do smell like crap. I don't know what a Jabberwocky is, but it must not be too pleasant if I smell like its ass. I file it away under the "Ask Hatter Later" section in my mind.

This time, I don't seem to have any trouble finding my way to my bedroom. There must be some sort of magic about it. As soon as I stop thinking too hard, and focus on the fact I want to go to my room, I wind up right in front of the purple door. When I walk inside, it's exactly the way I left it except that the bed is made. I certainly didn't make it. I look around the area briefly before going straight to the bathroom.

There's a large mirror above the sink, and I groan when I catch my reflection. I look like I took a tumble down a hill and then rolled in the mud for good measure. My hair is a massive pile of knots on top of my head, strands sticking out everywhere. There's blood splattered on my jacket, and I grimace. I don't even remember who or what's blood it can be. Was I standing close to the Bandersnatch when they were hit? Is it the Queen's blood? Is it mine? I have cuts on my cheeks from tree branches, so it can certainly be my blood. I turn away from the mirror.

I crank the water on for the tub, praising whatever deity is listening as hot water begins to pour from the faucet. There are various bottles lining the tub, and I sniff a few of them before deciding on one that smells like a mixture of Chamomile and chocolate. It's the same smell the Hatter gives off, and I wonder if he uses the same stuff. I pour a generous amount into the tub and watch the foam start to build up.

I unbutton the jacket and shrug it over my shoulders, grimacing at the muggy feel of my skin. It drops to the ground with a heavy thump. My shoulders instantly feel ten pounds lighter. I have to peel the leather pants off; they stick to my skin and make a sucking sound as I pull them down. I'm going to suggest that Dormouse burn the entire outfit, no matter how gorgeous it is. I don't think it can survive after all it has been through. The smell alone, I don't know if that'll ever come out.

Climbing into the froth-filled tub is heaven and then some. I sigh as the steaming water relaxes my weary muscles. I'm definitely getting my cardio in here in Wonderland. All this running has to be good for my thighs. I wash away the sweat, the grime, the blood from my skin before doing the same to my hair. The water turns dirty, and I have to let it out and refill it again, so I can lounge in it. The hot water feels nice as it runs over my blister-covered feet. I stay there, relaxing, until the water grows cold and my fingers wrinkle. The entire time, I think of nothing but the Hatter and his tortured soul. I want to help mend whatever is broken, but I don't know if I can. I don't know if I'm strong enough. I'm certainly going to try.

I wrap a large purple towel around me, humming a song as I walk from the bathroom. I let my hair hang loose around my shoulders, so it can air dry. When I see a certain cat lounging on my bed, I stop.

"Don't you know anything about privacy?" I ask, wrinkling my nose up at him.

"Of course," Cheshire replies. His tail is flicking back and forth. I'm not sure if he's agitated or feeling playful. He's sprawled out on my bed again, exactly like a cat. This man is more feline than human. He grins as he looks me up and down. I grip my towel tighter.

"Has anyone ever told you you're a creep?"

His grin widens impossibly.

"Yes."

I roll my eyes at his amusement.

"What are you doing here? Last I saw you, you had abandoned me to the Knave and disappeared with your tail between your legs."

It still rankles me that he had left me behind. He did warn me he was only out for himself. I guess it's really my fault for not listening. I should have expected it. I had trusted too easily. I won't do so again.

He flips over on his back, throwing his hands behind his head and stretching out further.

"Have you been to see the Caterpillar?" he drawls, ignoring my question.

I move towards the wardrobe Dormouse had mentioned and open it. Inside are yards and yards of different fabrics. I suck in a breath at the sheer number of outfits smashed inside. The bottom is lined with shoes. Where did all this come from? I can see everything from casual clothing to extravagant dresses. Why do I need all this?

I turn towards Cheshire again, studying him. The question had been loaded with something, some undertone of emotion that he hadn't wanted me to hear.

"Yes," I answer wearily.

"And what did you learn?"

"That I'm the first of the triad prophesied to bring down the Red Queen."

"And you're prepared for that?" he asks, studying his nails. "Are you prepared to fulfill a destiny written by someone else?"

"No." He looks up at me sharply, his eyes searching mine. "But I will do it."

"Why?"

It's such a simple question. One I'm not sure how to answer. Yes, I want to help Wonderland. Yes, I want to stop the Red Queen. But what business do I have saving a world that isn't even mine? Why am I okay with fulfilling a prophecy that was, indeed, written by someone else?

I glance at the doorway. I can't see him, but I can feel him. I don't know how, but there's a sort of connection between the Hatter and me. I have no idea when it happened, but it's there. And it seems I have my answer.

"Ahhh," Cheshire chuckles. "He's seduced you with his madness then?"

"No. He's awakened my curiosity."

"Curiosity killed the cat," Cheshire lectures, and he doesn't even laugh at the irony of him using the line. That grin stays locked on his face, though, so maybe it's a little funny to him. I'm beginning to wonder if the grin is a mask more than anything. "I suspect there's a bit more than curiosity."

My heart gives a hard throb at the truth in his words. I feel so much more for Hatter than simple curiosity. He's right. Wonderland is curious. It's inhabitants are curious. But the Hatter? The Hatter is a puzzle I keep trying to piece together, only to realize none of the pieces are from the same puzzle. He makes me burn, makes me love, makes me whole. I have to tell him that. I have to show him what he's beginning to mean to me. He is enough. He's enough exactly how he is, insanity and all.

Cheshire begins to fade from his place on the bed, his eyes sharp as they study me.

"Go to him," he urges before disappearing completely. I think he's gone when his final words echo through the room. "He needs you, Clara Bee."

I don't ask how he knows. I'm sure he's really gone this time. I don't suspect Cheshire as being too in touch with his feelings. The fact that he respects what I obviously feel for the Hatter throws me, and I realize that I'm again judging based on appearances. Never judge a book by its cover, or by the layer of Asshole attitude it uses to hide behind.

I put all thoughts of Cheshire from my mind. There's too many layers to him, and I just don't have the time to peel them all back. Curiouser and curiouser, that one.

I turn to the wardrobe.

Chapter 19

I rifle through the wardrobe, eventually stumbling upon a purple dress. It's short, shorter than anything I would normally wear, but I want to feel sexy, confident. I want to tempt. I zip myself into the dress, grateful it has a side zipper instead of a back one. The material is tight and strapless, hugging my hips and pushing my breasts up. When I look in the mirror, turning this way and that, I'm happy with the fit. I take the time to dry my hair, twisting the strands around my finger to give it a wave. It's the best I can do without a curling iron.

I find a pair of black heels in the wardrobe, too. They're easily five inches, giving me the height that'll bring me more level to the Hatter. I slip them on, fastening the little buckles on the side. I check myself in the mirror again and sigh. What am I doing? I'm dolling myself up for the Mad Hatter while I'm stuck in a twisted version of Wonderland. Oh! And I've almost died about four times now. And yet, all I seem to care about is if the Hatter will like the outfit or not. I brush away the thoughts, huffing at their direction. I'm not going to worry about the insanity of my situation right now. I'm going to focus on what I want and right now, that's the Hatter.

I walk from the room, heading for the stairs. The dress rides up, barely concealing the important bits. I tug at it nervously. My normal wardrobe consists of pant suits and pencil skirts. I haven't worn something this short since college, but I see the benefits. I feel sexy and confident. I feel powerful.

The sound of my heels clacking against the floor echoes

throughout the house as I carefully step down the staircase. Dormouse is nowhere to be seen. I strain my ears for any noise, but I hear nothing. It's eerily quiet, like I'm the only one home. Perhaps everyone disappears when the Hatter is in one of his moods.

I push open the doors of the ballroom, their creaking making me grimace. Good way to announce I'm coming in, I suppose. My eyes immediately go to the Hatter's chair, and I deflate when I find it empty. Sighing, I slowly make my way towards the end of the table, trailing my hand over the backs of the mismatched chairs. When I reach the Hatter's, I stare at it, admiring it. It's huge, more a throne than a simple chair. It's a matte black color, the arms and back carved with intricate designs of grotesque creatures and skulls. At the end of the arms, there's two skulls, perfectly placed to add an extra bit of menace. The cushions are a velvet purple material and look comfortable. The chair is scuffed up and worn, but it doesn't detract from it's impact. I suppose it makes sense for the Hatter to have a throne. He's the King of Tea Time, after all.

I tug my skirt down and sit in the chair, attempting to get comfortable. The tea cups in front of me are empty, the cakes normally piled on the plates are gone. I guess those are saved for actual tea parties. I never realized they aren't here all the time. I cross my legs and stare at the empty cups, my thoughts running away with possibility.

The prophecy states I will be the one to bring down the Knave and win the Hatter's heart, but it doesn't say what I'm supposed to do after that. Am I supposed to stay in Wonderland and forget my old life? What about my clients, my job . . . . I stop myself. What do I really have to go back to? Sure, I have a job I love, but that's it. I have no real friends, no family. I chose to focus on work, instead. I don't have anyone to tie me down, my parents long since having passed away. I don't even have a pet to worry about since I work such long hours. What do I really, honestly have to go back to? Do I even want to go back?

I'm so lost in thought, I don't hear anyone enter the ballroom. I'm taken completely by surprise when a hand comes from nowhere and wraps around my neck. I freeze but the hand doesn't tighten. It doesn't hurt me. When the Hatter steps into view beside me, I realize exactly why that is. I look up at him in awe. He isn't wearing his normal jacket, only the top hat and his leather pants. The necklace he always wears dangles between his pecs. I eye his abs in appreciation before jerking my eyes back to his face.

"Why are you in my chair?" There's a thread of menace in his voice that does things low in my belly.

"I was looking for you," I breathe.

His eyes follow the movement of my chest, locked on the view of my breasts threatening to spill from the dress. His eyes darken when they take in the rest of my outfit, the barely there coverage, the skin I'm showing. The breath whistles from between his teeth. His jaw clenches.

"Stand up," he commands, his hand leaving my neck.

I do as he says, wobbling a bit in the heels. The Hatter is eying me, setting a fire inside I have no desire to smother. He takes my place in his seat, getting comfortable before he reaches out and snags my wrist. He tugs until I step forward. He reaches out and effortlessly picks me up by my waist before placing me on his lap, my legs spread around his. The dress is so short, it has nowhere to go but up, and I can feel how exposed I am. Do I care? Not one bit. As I straddle his hips, his hands clench hard on my own, his eyes riveted to where my dress bunches up. His pupils dilate.

"Clara Bee, oh, Clara Bee, what is it you're doing to me?" His voice is rough, tormented. When his eyes slam into mine, I smile.

I reach up and pluck the top hat from his head. I'm tempted to put it on again, to tease. Instead, I set it gently down in the closest chair. I wrap my arms around Hatter's neck, my fingers tangling in the hair at his nape. I scrape my nails there, pleased when he shivers. I can feel his arousal between my legs, pressing against me. I just barely stop myself from rubbing on him like a cat.

I summon the little bit of bravery I had before I came downstairs and speak.

"Hatter, I'm in trouble it seems, I believe you promised to make me scream." I stare deep into his eyes as I say it, so he doesn't miss what I mean. I bite my lip when his quirk up into a smile.

His hands leave my hips, wrapping around me to grab my ass tight, pushing me down on his hardness. A breath whooshes out of me at the feeling of us grinding together. I use my nails a little harder on the back of his neck, and his hands spasm at my back side.

I throw any hesitation I had to the wind. I lean forward, trailing my tongue up his neck, kissing him along the way. He growls, the sound vibrating through his body as his hands grind me harder against him. The feeling is exquisite, but it's not nearly enough. I want everything he can give me.

I trail my lips back down, stopping at the muscle between his shoulder and his neck. I hover there for a moment before biting down, hard, on the sensitive spot. Hatter snarls and then the world tilts. I'm confused until I hear the tea cups on the table scatter, hitting the floor and breaking into hundreds of pieces. More china suffers the same fate as Hatter lays me down on the wooden surface. He keeps my legs hooked around his waist as he looks at me, his hands spreading trails of fire as they caress my thighs. The necklace dangles down from his chest, floating above me. It has an odd symbol on it, but this isn't the time to ask or study.

"You shouldn't have done that." His hands move from gentle to a little rough as he grabs me tight. He yanks on my body, the action slamming my core against his hardness. The only barriers are his pants and my lace thong. My breath stutters when he comes down on top of me. I try to wrap my arms around his neck, but he grips my wrists tight in his hand before pinning them above my head. He nips at my shoulders and neck, leaving behind little stings that he soothes with his tongue.

"Hatter," I moan, rubbing against him.

He moves back enough to look down into my face, his eyes a bit wild.

"Are you sure?" he asks, his hesitation breaking through the moment. Even now, he worries about me.

"If you stop, I will never forgive you," I groan.

He grins, leaning forward to capture my mouth in his. The kiss is fiery and passionate, all the built up emotions we've been putting off spilling past our lips. He keeps my hands pinned over my head, but his other hand slides up my side, before sliding along the neckline of the dress.

"Such a pretty dress," he mumbles into my mouth right before he grips at my cleavage and pulls. He tugs with such force, the dress rips down the middle, but it doesn't come off. It only rips enough to reveal my breasts. The purple material stays wrapped around my middle, the skirt having long since ridden up my waist. "Better." He palms my breasts in his hand, his fingers pinching my nipple. I moan into his mouth, breathing hard. I shift, trying to rub against what I want, but he moves away, leaving a gap between us. I groan in protest. "Patience, Clara Bee," he teases. "I've waited a long time for you." He take his hand from my wrists but not before he mutters a stern, "Don't move."

He slides down my body, his hands caressing. He pauses over my breasts before leaning forward and catching one nipple between his lips.

"Oh," I moan, my thighs clenching around him.

He releases it with a pop before continuing down. When I think he's going to keep trailing kisses, he pulls from between my legs and sits down completely. I lift my head and look at him in confusion.

"What are you doing?" I ask, frowning at the loss of his weight.

His eyes trail over me, his angle letting him see everything, letting him see me laid out on the table.

"Admiring the view," he replies, grinning. "If only tea time was this beautiful." I blush, laying my head back down. "Look at you," he continues, "all spread out in front of me like a feast."

His words shoot to my core, and I try to close my thighs, to hide. It's more instinct than anything else. His hands grab my knees, preventing me from closing them completely.

"Hatter." My voice is husky, breathy.

He hums, his eyes crinkling as he notices my discomfort. His hands begin trailing up my legs, starting from the heels strapped to my feet. I never thought fingers lightly trailing across my ankles and then my calves would be such a turn on, but by the time his fingers reach my knees, I'm jelly in his hands.

"There's a lot about me you probably don't understand," he says, pausing his movements when his fingers reach my knees. "There's a lot that I don't show to anyone." His fingers move again, barely trailing up my inner thigh, moving excruciatingly slow. "I'm chaos, Clara Bee." His eyes meet mine when I look at him again. "I'm chaos, and I'll destroy you."

"I'm not afraid of you," I tell him, and it's the truth. He's intense and deadly, but he's also mine, destined to be with me. I'm not afraid of him. I know him better than he thinks I do. His darkness calls to my own.

"You should be," he replies, his fingers tracing the edge of my thong. "You should be afraid to be at my mercy."

I smile at him, letting him see everything written on my face.

"Don't hold back." His eyes widen, surprised, but he moves past it quickly.

His face darkens as he slips beneath the lace, and his fingers finally, blessedly, touch exactly where I want him to. His eyes don't leave mine as he slides into the slickness pooling between my thighs. My chest rises and falls fast, oxygen in short supply.

He reaches forward and rips the thong from me, the flimsy material snapping apart easily to leave me bare before him.

"So beautiful," he says. He's still sitting in the chair with me spread in front of him. I'm surprised when he leans forward. I cry out when his lips close around my clit, sucking hard. My hips lift from the table, and his hands reach up to slam them back down again, holding me against the surface while he feasts on me.

"Fuck," I groan, my hands unable to stay above my head. I reach down and thread them through his hair. I knock another teacup off as I do, the shatter barely penetrating the haze of passion.

Hatter turns his head to the side and bites my inner thigh, making me jump in surprise.

"I told you not to move your hands," he growls.

I throw my hands back over my head, gripping them tight. He licks up my seam slowly as a reward, alternating between nipping and using his tongue. One hand releases my hip and slips down, his finger sliding through the moisture while he focuses on my clit. The finger slips inside, and I mew. When he adds another, I begin moving, trying to get closer. I feel him grin against me.

"So impatient," he chuckles before kissing my core. He stands, his fingers leaving me. I feel empty for a moment, but I don't complain when I hear a zip. I look up at him, watching as he pushes his leather pants down to reveal his cock, standing proud. I bite my lip in anticipation. "Last chance, Clara Bee," he says, his eyes heated as they trace my body. "If we do this, I'll never get enough of you."

"Don't stop," I whisper, meeting his eyes. "Give me everything."

He growls. "You don't want everything."

"I do." Our eyes stay locked. "I want everything you have to give. Hold nothing back."

He growls again, the sound more savage than before, and he steps between my legs, hooking mine around his waist. I'm already hanging slightly off the edge of the table, at the perfect angle. I hold my breath as he lines up, his face wild, but he doesn't push in, doesn't give me what I want. I groan in frustration.

"Fuck me already," I snarl.

That grin spreads across his face, the one that's a tiny bit psycho. "There's that darkness," he says with glee. Then he slams inside of me, and I scream out in pleasure, my legs clenching around him. He pauses for a moment, ecstasy on his face as he looks down at me.

I shift my hips, moving my hands again to wrap around his neck. He bites down on my breast before pulling out and slamming back in. My breath skips, my nails clenching hard onto his shoulders. There's a rattle when he slams into me again and another crash somewhere in the distance. His lips crush mine, and I can taste myself as I kiss him back frantically. Our teeth clack as we fight to get closer.

One hand wraps gently around my neck again, and he begins to piston in and out of me. I cry out in pleasure, my mind fleeing under the onslaught. He's rough and brutal, not slowing his pace, but I wouldn't have it any other way. He's giving me everything. He's giving me his soul.

He straightens, gripping my ankles in his hand and bending them back, putting my knees towards my chest. He reached deeper inside me, hitting right on my g-spot each time. I'm frantic with pleasure, my hands having nothing to clench onto as he powers into me.

"Fuck," he groans when I grab my breasts, kneading them hard. "You're everything, Clara Bee," he growls before pulling out. He jerks me to my feet. My legs won't hold me up under the sudden rush of blood, but I don't have to worry. He turns me around quickly and pushes down on my back until I'm bent over the table. His hand grips my hair tight in his fist before he slams into me again. This time, I scream out in pleasure. He doesn't slow, doesn't go gentle as he claims me right there on his famous table, dishes breaking as they rattle off and hit the floor.

Hatter pulls up on my hair, until my back arches, and he can wrap his hand around my neck again. I turn my head, and his lips capture mine, his pace never slowing. He pushes my hair to the side, nipping where my shoulder meets my neck, before biting down, marking me. I explode, my climax taking me by surprise, a cry of absolute pleasure echoing around the empty ballroom. His hand barely tightens on my neck, squeezing just a hint as I clench around him. His rhythm stutters, his chest rumbling with another growl as he thrusts into me a few more times before he tumbles after me, his warmth dripping down my thighs. I'm thankful I have an IUD inserted. I don't think I will ever be able to remember a condom where the Hatter is involved. All my sensibilities go out the window.

Our breathing slows, but we don't move, still intertwined, my back to his chest. His arms support me, keeping me from puddling to the floor.

"You're perfect," Hatter whispers in my ear. "You're absolutely perfect."

I shift, turning in his arms as he slips out of me. I lean back on the table, letting it support my weight as I grasp his cheeks between my hands.

"And you're everything," I tell him. "You are enough, and I wouldn't change you for the world."

His eyes glisten before he closes his eyes and leans his forehead against mine. His hands rest at my hips.

"Do you mean that?" he whispers, and I feel tears spring to my eyes. He is so damaged, so tortured. He thinks he isn't worth what I have to give, and nothing could be further from the truth. I'm more worried I'm not enough for him.

I kiss him on the tip of his nose.

"I'm falling hard for you, Hatter, and it has nothing to do with a prophecy. I feel that way because of who you are, not who everyone else paints you to be. I see you. And I want you."

He picks me up from the table suddenly. I squeak and wrap my legs around his waist.

"Where are we going?" I ask as he begins to walk with me in his arms.

"My room."

"Wait! We can't walk through the house like this! I'm naked."

Technically, I'm still wearing the dress, but it's around my waist. The tear is bigger than I thought, going down all the way to my navel, so the whole thing just sort of hangs off of me. He stops, looking speculatively at my state of undress.

"You're right," he says, setting me gently on my feet again. I'm able to stand by myself this time as he goes behind his chair and comes back with his purple jacket. He holds it out for me to slide into. I breath in the scent that comes from it, chocolate and chamomile, the smell that always accompanies him. I grab his top hat and hand it to him. Instead of putting it on, he plops it on my head. When I look at him in question, he grins.

"I like seeing you in my clothing," he shrugs. "In my room, I expect you to wear nothing but those heels and my hat."

Desire flickers through my abdomen, ready to go again even after the intense session we just had. I'll no doubt be sore tomorrow.

As the Hatter wraps his arm around me and leads me from the room, glass crunching under our shoes, I throw every thought out of my head. I can worry about Wonderland and the prophecy tomorrow. For today, I'm going to get lost in my Hatter.

Oh, how I wish I can stay lost forever.

Chapter 20

Another tea party calls us away from each other's arms the next morning. We were so wrapped up in each other that we didn't hear Dormouse knocking on the door, alerting us. It isn't until he slams his fist against the door repeatedly that we break apart. I sit up in a panic in the bed, clutching the purple silk sheets to my chest. Hatter laughs, his wandering hands tugging at it gently.

"Knock it off," I hiss. "Dormouse can hear us."

"It's time for tea." Dormouse's bored voice carries through the wooden door. "I'll expect you two in thirty minutes."

I blanch, the fact that Dormouse knows what we're getting up to behind the closed door freaking me out. I hear him walk away, the floorboards creaking under his measured steps.

"Oh my God. He knows."

Hatter sits up and pulls me back on the bed again. He braces himself on his elbow above me, smiling.

"Dormouse will never dare speak a word of it. He's far too stiff for that."

"How am I supposed to look him in the eyes again?" I worry my bottom lip, my hands sliding up the Hatter's side. I trail my nails over his ribs.

"I'm positive everyone in Wonderland will know and expect that we share a bed. Dormouse has probably expected it from the beginning."

My eyes widen.

"All of Wonderland knows..."

"All of Wonderland knew of the Hatter's mate the moment the prophecy spoke our fate," he sings, kissing the tip of my nose.

"Great. Good to know everyone knows our sex life." There's no shame in my words. In fact, the more I think about it, the sillier it seems to worry. I wrap my arms around the Hatter's neck.

"I can make you forget about it," the Hatter teases, his eyes sparkling at me.

"But we'll be late for tea."

"Ah, yes. Tea time." His words are sad for a moment before he perks up. "All I need is two minutes to make you forget." He grins.

I wrap my legs around his waist.

"I'll give you five."

I retreat to my own room to get ready, stealing a robe that had been hanging on the Hatter's door. He watched me from the bed, his skin as slick as mine with sweat. He'd been completely naked, lounging across the sheets, his hat covering his important bits, teasing me. It's an image I have a hard time getting out of my brain, so I can focus on the task at hand.

My heels dangle from my fingertips, my feet bare as I open my door and slip inside the quiet room. I lean back against the wood, a goofy smile on my face. I'm sore in all the right places, making me forget the aches from all the running. I'm not sore enough to cause any trouble in a fight, but it's enough to remind me what I had been up to all night.

"You look like you've been enjoying yourself."

I scowl as Cheshire takes shape, this time leaning against the post of my bed.

"Seriously?" I toss my heels off to the side, a soft thunk echoing when they land on the carpet. "Don't you know how to knock?"

He shrugs. "Why would I knock when I can just come in?"

I shake my head. There's no hope for the man. He just doesn't seem to care about privacy. Why he insists on torturing me, I have no idea. I'm gonna have to remember never to walk around naked in my room. My eyes widen.

"You haven't been spying on me while I'm in other places, have you?"

His lips curl up in a half smile.

"Relax. I haven't been watching whatever it is you and the Hatter have been up to."

I breathe a sigh of relief before crossing my arms over my chest.

"What do you want, Cheshire?"

"I have a question for you."

When he doesn't elaborate, I raise my eyebrow.

"Well?"

His face grows serious. I start thinking he isn't going to ask when he finally straightens and meets my eyes.

"The Hatter obviously cares for you. Do you feel the same for him?"

"Of course, I care about the Hatter. Why do you ask?"

"Is it because you know you're destined to be? Is it because of the prophecy that you care about him?"

It dawns on me. Cheshire is fishing, and he's worried. Absolem had said Cheshire is the third Son of Wonderland, though I suspected as much before he confirmed it. Cheshire is destined to find a mate that completes the triad, the third woman who will help me and another to bring down the Red Queen.

I notice Cheshire is fidgeting, his tail swishing back and forth, his fingers tapping a rhythm on his thigh. He's trying his hardest to appear cool and indifferent, but I'm starting to see a little beneath his mask. I can choose not to answer his question. It's personal, after all. But when I open my mouth, I find the truth tumbles out without hesitation.

"I'll admit there was a draw there at the beginning. It's kind of like this feeling in your chest, tugging at you even though you're wary, or scared. I was curious about it, sure." I walk across the room and stand in front of him. I look into his eyes, the pupils moving between a circle and a slit, like he can't decide which look to assume. "But, that didn't force me to love the Hatter. The Hatter captured my heart all on his own. No prophecy did that."

"You speak of love," he whispers in awe. His tail finally stops moving as he stares back at me. "How can you know that it isn't some greater force messing with your emotions?"

"You can't force people to love. If that was the case, when I first saw the Hatter, I wouldn't have felt fear, or worry, or confusion. There was no instant love. I can tell you the exact moment that it happened, and it wasn't at first sight."

"It wasn't?"

"No. It was at the March Hare's house, after I drank the Reali-Tea, minutes before the Bandersnatch howled outside. March was being March." I chuckle at the image of him rolling on the floor laughing. "I had just seen the terrible history of the Red Queen, I was covered in a cold sweat, and I was crying. And you know what happened?"

"What?"

"The Hatter told me I'm his light inside the Madness. That I'm the light that brings him home." I smile, remembering the words. "I fell in love right there. Those words sealed my fate. That was the moment I embraced it." Cheshire looks up at the ceiling for a moment. I take his hand, just holding on to give him comfort. The touch brings his eyes back to me, his eyebrows crinkled in confusion. It gives his face an innocent look, one that he would never normally wear. "I understand if the idea of a destined mate scares you, Cheshire. But this is the way I see it: The prophecy knows which two people are compatible, sure. But it's up to you whether the love grows from that or not. You decide whether you want to embrace that fate. No one else does."

"No woman could ever look at me the way you look at Hatter, Clara." His voice is sad, accepting, and I hear the brokenness inside them. "Besides," he shrugs, "I don't believe in all that love shit."

That quickly, he dismisses everything I had said, the hope in his eyes blinking away. I smile, giving his hand a light squeeze. His eyes change to those of a cat as he looks at me. It doesn't unnerve me anymore. He's trying to erect his mask of indifference back into place, but it's too late. I can already see past it.

"You will," I assure him. "When you see her."

He doesn't respond to the comment, but he begins to fade away. His hand slips from mine as his body disappears. His face is the last to go.

"I'll see you at tea, Clara Bee," his voice echoes before his glowing blue eyes disappear completely.

There is another outfit laid out on my bed, similar to the first. Leather pants, yet again in black, are sitting on top. The top is black this time, a pretty golden damask pattern on it, and much lower cut than the high neck of the first jacket. It'll show some cleavage and make it less stuffy. It's sleeveless, stopping at the tops of my shoulders. The back of the jacket is less formal than the first one. It only goes down to my knees, and it looks more like long coat tails than the back half of a skirt. There's a different pair of combat boots to complement the outfit, a weathered gold color. I put the ensemble on before tying my hair up in a messy bun. I strap all the weapons back onto my body, stumbling over which way to fasten the buckles, and head downstairs for the ballroom. Again, it's easier to maneuver through the house. I have no trouble finding my way.

When I reach the ballroom, it's Dormouse who opens the heavy door for me. I can't meet his eyes, my face turning a nice shade of red, but I shouldn't have worried. He doesn't meet mine either, ever the face of professionalism. As I step through the doors, the guests of the tea party stop talking, their eyes all focusing on me. I pause.

I jump when Dormouse speaks behind me, shouting at Cheshire who is already sitting down towards the head of the table, close to the Hatter.

"Get your feet off the table, you uncultured Grimalkin," Dormouse sneers. It's the most emotion I've ever heard come from him, his offense at bad manners strong.

Cheshire grins at him, but he doesn't remove his boots where they sit propped up on the table top. Dormouse scoffs and slams the door closed behind him as he leaves.

Tweedledee and Tweedledum are sitting side by side about midway down the table. Their heads are tilted together as they study the guests. There's equal parts hunger and curiosity on their faces. I make a mental note to ask Hatter if we should be worried about that or not. I hate to think I have to tell them every time that the guests are friends. Maybe I'll make a sign and hang it on the wall. Has the Hatter been feeding them? I think hard and realize I don't remember them ever eating. Do they eat food, or, something more horrifying? It goes into the "Ask Hatter" file in my brain.

White sits beside Cheshire, his face clouded with anger. He keeps checking his watch over and over again. When he looks up at my entrance, he throws his hands in the air, and I swear I hear the word "finally". His ears twitch in agitation, his knuckles rapping against the table top.

There are other guests as well, those of the deceased. There's more than I have ever seen at once. I count fourteen this time. Fourteen more creatures and people have died by the Queen's hand. She's increasing the amount, probably because we had escaped her. She must be so angry that we got away, that the Caterpillar helped us.

Hatter sits in his normal chair, his eyes sparkling when they watch me walk into the ballroom. My face reddens as I make my way down the table to my chair, especially when I think about the things we had done on this very spot only last night. Hatter smiles wickedly, like he knows exactly why I'm turning red. I get flashes of skin, visions of the last time we used the table.

"There's less china than there usually is," Cheshire comments, studying the table. "What happened to the sugar bowl? I like sugar in my tea."

I can't help it. A small chuckle slips out, my face reddening even more. I'm sure I look like a tomato. Cheshire's eyes catch on mine, and his eyebrows go up. He leans back away from the table, removing his feet and eying it suspiciously, like he's checking for evidence.

"Fitting for the Hatter," he mumbles. Thankfully, no one else seems to understand our conversation. I can't bear that conversation.

I'm about to take my seat when the Hatter slips his arm around my waist and pulls me into his lap, sprawling me in an awkward position. I laugh and adjust myself to one side, making it easier for both of us to see the table and our guests. I wrap one arm behind his neck, my fingers playing with the chain there.

"You look maddeningly ravishing in the clothes I picked for you," he whispers in my ear, his hands wrapping around my stomach and rubbing, teasing.

"Everyone is watching," I hiss.

"Let them watch."

My face heats even more, but I don't fight him, too giddy. Besides, I don't actually want him to stop. White is watching us closely, curiosity on his face. Cheshire is purposely ignoring us.

"So, does anyone have a plan?" I venture, the hum in the room dying as they all focus on me again. No one answers. "To defeat the Knave," I clarify. Maybe they don't understand what I'm asking.

"You could always just lop off his head," Cheshire supplies, studying his claws. "Simple enough really."

"I'd like to avoid that if possible. The Knave is just as much a victim as we are. If there is a way to save him, I'd prefer to do that." I look around at the silent guests. Tweedledum and Tweedledee watch me, both eerily still.

"Some people might be too far gone to be saved," the Hatter speaks, his voice loud enough, so the room hears. I turn to look at him, meeting his eyes. There's sadness there.

"Do you really believe that?" I ask. "Do you believe there are those of you who can't be saved?"

"Not too long ago," White interrupts, "you didn't think you could be saved, Hatter."

Hatter tilts his head at White in acknowledgment before looking at me again.

"So, we need a plan that involves saving the prince," Hatter agrees. "No pressure."

"Why do we need to eliminate the prince?" someone down the table asks, a woman with horns. "Why not just go for the Red Queen? Take out the Queen, and everything else is a moot point."

"The Knave is the Red Queen's general. He must be removed so that she is weakened," the Hatter replies. "The prophecy speaks of the triad. Clara is only the first. The Caterpillar says there is only one possible future where we succeed. This is that future."

When no one else speaks, I turn to the Tweedles.

"Is there a way to reverse what the Red Queen has done to the Prince?" I word my question carefully, specifying all the people in question. Less chance of them leading me astray that way.

As part of our deal, they're supposed to supply council and advice. No doubt they repeat the deal in their heads before deciding to answer. They do nothing without consulting each other first. They also do nothing without getting something in return.

"There are ways," Dee says.

"It might work if it did," Dum adds.

"It might fail if it doesn't," Dee finishes.

I see a shudder run through a few of the guests. It seems I'm not the only one creeped out by the twins.

"It'll be risky then." I nod, meeting Dum's eyes, getting used to the way they speak. "What must be done in order to save him?"

Everything has a price in Wonderland. If I want to save the Prince, there will be a fair trade. I need to know if I can pay it. They speak at the same time, that eerie voice floating through the air.

"Love brought about the Prince's demise. Love will set him free."

I look at the Hatter.

"Who did the Prince love?" I ask, even though I have a sneaking suspicion.

"Only one as far as I know," he mumbles. "Alice."

I sigh.

"Great. So that's a no go. Maybe it doesn't have to be romantic love. Maybe it could be Maternal love?"

Hatter's face lights up, excitement coursing through him as he tenses beneath me.

"The Queen!" he exclaims. "He loved the Queen."

"His mother," Cheshire clarifies. "How can his mother help bring him back? She's dead."

"I might be able to act as a beacon of some sort, able to tether the Queen to this world in the same way I was able to tether Clara in the Hereafter."

"You did that?" White asks, startled. "You've never done that before."

"Change came to Wonderland, the moment Clara Bee linked our hands," Hatter says, shrugging.

"Will she be able to do it? Would she want to?" I ask, happy to have some sort of plan in place.

"There's only one way to find out." Hatter lifts me from the chair, setting me on my feet. "Tea party is over everyone. It's time to go."

The guests stand up and begin making their way towards the other side of the room. The twins eye them and stand up. I see Dee lick her lips. I'm starting to think Tweedledum and Tweedledee eat souls.

"They're friends," I tell them again, just to put it out there in case they're trying to pull the we didn't know card. "Everyone in this house at this moment is a friend." I'm definitely putting up a sign.

They sigh in disappointment before taking their seats again. They sip their tea in silence, their attention on me.

Be warned, Dee's voice floats through my head.

The Hereafter may take a life from the living, Dum adds.

If you take a soul from the dead.

Great. Nothing to stress out about then, I think. I hope it doesn't come to that. And I seriously hope the Tweedles never speak in my mind again. They leave behind an oily feeling. It makes me want to scrape the inside of my brain out.

Cheshire and White still sit at the table, watching us. White checks his watch again, his knee bouncing restlessly. Cheshire grins when he notices me staring.

"Try not to get lost." The message is clear. I scowl at his tasteless comment, steeling my spine as we float towards the other side of the room. When I look over my shoulder, both of them are focused elsewhere.

"Are you ready, Clara Bee?" Hatter asks. I nod even though my hands shake. The last time hadn't been so fun; we barely made it out in time.

He wraps my hand in his, throws his hat, and the portal opens before us.

"Next time we come here, remind me to wear shorts and a tank top," I huff as the humidity hits me. Sweat immediately beads on my forehead, my leather pants and jacket making it almost unbearable.

"You could always take the clothes off." Hatter grins and wiggles his eyebrows. I roll my eyes.

"Yes, exactly what I want to do. Meet the former Queen of Wonderland while naked."

"Suit yourself." He shrugs his jacket off and drapes it over his shoulder, all while keeping our skin touching. Shirtless and wearing nothing but leather pants, boots, and his hat, the Hatter is a sight to behold, especially while his body glistens with sweat. I frown at how easy it is for him to take his jacket off and glance down at my own, contemplating. I had saved my white cami I had been wearing beneath my clothes when I fell down the rabbit hole. I had put it on this morning, just to give an extra barrier between the jacket and my skin. It's thin, and it will no doubt show everything through the flimsy material, but it's ridiculously hot, and I'm pretty sure I'm going to start melting soon if I don't do something.

"Fine," I mutter, working on the buttons down the front of the jacket.

Hatter pauses, watching me with rapt interest as I slip the jacket from my shoulders, revealing the translucent cami underneath. The sweat has made it even worse, outlining my lace bra underneath. His eyes heat when they drop to the shadow of my nipples through the fabric.

"Maybe you should leave it on," he strains, wiping his forehead with the back of his arm.

"It's hot," I point out. "You should have dressed me in something cooler if you wanted me to keep it on."

"I might just back you against a tree and have my way with you." His voice is husky, and it warms my core when the images immediately jump into my brain. He shakes his head, like he's trying to dislodge the thought. "We're on borrowed time. No time for a dalliance in the Hereafter." He looks at my chest again. "But later. Later, later, later." He smiles.

We begin moving through the jungle. I try to stay focused on the task at hand, but it's difficult with the vibes coming from the Hatter. They're hard to ignore. Between his sideways looks and the "accidental" brushes against my heated body as we weave through the trees, it's almost impossible to pretend there isn't such thick tension buzzing between us. I repeat the same words in my mind over and over again. We don't have time. We don't have time. The tips of my fingers are already fading.

"So, where exactly do we find the Queen in a jungle?" I'm thankful I had the foresight to tie my hair up in a loose bun. The sweat runs down my neck in steady trails. I'm not used to this kind of humidity. I don't see how anyone could be, honestly. It's like a sauna.

"Follow the trail of a thousand tears to fancy a meeting with the Old Queen's ears."

I frown at the Hatter.

"What does that mean? The trail of a thousand tears?"

He doesn't answer, instead pointing to the ground in our path. It's the first time I notice a little sparkle there, something reflecting the light of the sun at increments. It kind of looks like glitter. I bend down, keeping my hand in Hatter's and take a closer look at what's causing the light refractions.

"It's a crystal," I say, shocked. "A bunch of crystals."

"Diamonds."

A strangled choke comes from my throat.

"We're following a trail of diamonds. Holy shit!"

And these diamonds are like nothing I've ever seen before. They shine more than I've ever seen a diamond shine, their facets refracting the light like a star. I have no idea how I missed them before.

"You have to know what to look for," Hatter says, answering my unspoken thoughts. "If you don't know they're there, you won't see them."

"How is that possible?"

He shrugs. "Magic, I suppose."

It's a Wonderland answer, one I don't really understand, but I no longer question. There are just some things beyond my comprehension.

We continue through the dense jungle, the sound of animals chattering around us. I still don't see anyone even though I expect there to be thousands of creatures and people here.

"Where are all the people?" I ask, curious. Shouldn't the Hereafter be more populated?

"You have to look closer. The Hereafter only shows you what you want to see. You have to want to see everyone to be able to see it."

"Okay." I pinch my lips in concentration. "I have to want to see them," I repeat to myself. I think about meeting people around me, about seeing the inhabitants.

Suddenly, everything becomes clearer, and we're no longer walking through a lifeless jungle. We're surrounded by creatures all around us, following our trail. Pink monkey-like creatures hop from tree branch to tree branch, keeping their pace beside us. There's a porcupine and some sort of green-striped cat walking beside me. As I stare at them in wonder, the green cat lifts its face to mine and human eyes stare back, startling me so badly, I trip. The Hatter keeps me upright. As I watch, the cat shifts, turning into a woman before my eyes. Her hair is as green as her coat was, her dress a nice shade of gold. Large ears sit on her head, a tail behind her, just like Cheshire. The only difference is that where Cheshire is all blue, she's all green.

"Hatter," she exclaims, beaming widely. "So good of you to visit."

"Danica," Hatter smiles sadly. "It's nice to see you again."

"And you must be Clara," she says, focusing on me. "I've heard the chatter. I'm happy I get to meet you. I just wish it was in the land of the living rather than here."

"It's nice to meet you," I tell her, smiling. I like her instantly. She has this innocent air about her; it makes me want to protect her even if she doesn't need it, even if it's long past overdue.

"There's so much that has changed, Hatter. One day soon, you and Clara must come visit for tea." She grins at him, a mischievous look on her face.

"We'd be delighted," he replies. I smile and nod my head.

"Well, I have to go," Danica says, smiling sweetly at us. "Will you tell Cheshire I said hello?" She turns but hesitates. "And tell him I love him and to stay out of trouble."

Hatter snorts.

"Cheshire doesn't stay out of trouble. You know that."

"Just tell him. Maybe hearing it from me will make a difference."

Hatter nods and Danica transforms back into a cat.

Give Wonderland hell, Clara, her voice floats through my mind. *Take her down for all of us.*

It startles me—seriously, can everyone speak in my mind in Wonderland?—but I smile that I understand. When she's gone, I turn to the Hatter again.

"Who is she to Cheshire?"

He looks at the canopy above us, watching the birds fluttering around, the pink monkeys swinging from branch to branch.

"His little sister," he whispers so softly I barely catch it.

My heart stops.

"Oh no," I mumble. "Was it the Red Queen?"

He doesn't respond right away, but he doesn't have to. I already know the answer. It makes me angry, so angry, that the Red Queen has taken so much from Wonderland. All for ill-placed revenge.

"She must be stopped," Hatter says as we begin moving again. "At all costs."

"I agree." I squeeze his hand gently in mine. "We'll take her down."

He looks at me, his eyes incredibly sad. I can't imagine the burden of passing those you care about to the Hereafter, watching them die one by one at the hands of someone you once called friend. The Hatter is the strongest person I have ever met.

And I love him even more for it.

I know we're close when I start smelling roses. That is my first sign. The next is the smoke that whispers alongside it, like someone is cooking outside. When we break through the trees, the trail of diamonds ending, my eyes fall on a quaint little cabin. The roses grow up the side of it, pure white in color. There isn't a single speck of red, and I understand why those in the Hereafter wouldn't want to see the flowers ever again.

"I expected something bigger," I tell Hatter honestly. They were the King and Queen after all, living in a castle. This is a considerable downsize, even if it looks comfortable and cute. There's a fire going in the yard, some kind of creature roasting over the flame. I can't tell what it is, but it kind of looks like a giant turkey.

"The late King and Queen have always been modest. They were known for being very generous and made sure no one ever went hungry. If you didn't have somewhere to eat dinner, anyone was welcome to walk in their doors and join their table."

"Exactly how a ruler should be." I smile at the thought, wishing more people were like them. It sounds like they were the perfect monarchs.

The front door opens, and the woman from my brush with Reali-tea steps through. She's wearing a simple yellow dress and a gold circlet across her forehead. She still looks as regal as she did in her full court gown, her posture giving her status away. Her face lights up when she sees Hatter. She rushes across the yard and wraps him in a warm hug. I'm tugged along with the embrace since our hands are still locked together. My opposite arm has already completely faded, and my leg is right behind it. The queen releases the Hatter, and her eyes fall on me.

"Is this her?" she asks the Hatter in wonder.

"I'm Clara," I supply helpfully, and the woman squeals in excitement before wrapping me in her arms. It cuts off my breath, it's so tight.

"I'm so happy I get to meet the woman who had won our dear Hatter's heart." I blush, tucking a few stray hairs away from my face when she lets me go. "Edward is out helping some of the newest inhabitants build homes. But please come inside. Join me for tea."

"I'm afraid we don't have much time, your majesty." Hatter smiles sadly. "How I wish we could stay, but Clara doesn't belong here, and she's fading. If we don't make it back before she fades completely, I might lose her forever."

"Oh dear! We don't want that! Is there something I can do for you then? You didn't come to the Hereafter to risk her life for nothing."

"No," I interject. I look at the Hatter, and he nods in encouragement. "We need your help."

Her face hardens.

"I'm afraid I won't be able to lift my sword and fight anymore. If that's what you're after."

"The prophecy says I'm to be the downfall of the Knave," I say quietly.

"My son." Her face is grave as she listens to me closely, hanging on my every word.

"Yes, but Alexander is a victim in all of this no matter what he's done under the influence of the Red Queen. If I can save him without killing him, I would prefer to do that."

She blinks at me before gently cupping my cheeks in her hands. Her eyes glisten.

"I thank you for that, Clara. You are everything I imagined you would be." She lets me go and puts her hands on her hips. "Now tell me how I play into all this."

"The Tweedles–" She scoffs at the Hatter, and I suspect it's because of a dislike for the twins. "–have said that love can set him free," Hatter continues after her interruption.

"Alice is a dead end, of course," I add.

"But you want me to try?" The queen is pensive. "They didn't specify what kind of love?"

"No. Only that it must be love."

"You're quite clever to jump to the conclusion of maternal love, dear." The queen smiles. "Of course, I'm willing to help. Let me just leave a note for Edward, and we can be on our way before I start worrying. You're turning quite translucent."

"You'll be tethered to me in Wonderland, your majesty. You'll be present but incorporeal," the Hatter tells her. Maybe now is a good time to mention the Tweedles' warning? I watch them carefully and shake my head. If there's a price to pay, I'll pay it. Anything to stop the Red Queen.

"I understand." She turns to me. "You really think my love can break him from the prison of his mind?"

I meet her eyes.

"I think it's worth a shot. If I can save your son, I will."

She smiles fondly at me before rushing inside to leave a note. When she returns, we make the trek back through the jungle, the animals once again chattering and following us. The queen talks with them sweetly, urging them to come forward and sit on her shoulders.

I find myself wishing she was still the queen, still the ruler of Wonderland. But then, I look at Hatter, so determined to save his world, fighting the madness that creeps into his soul, and I thank

Mad as a Hatter

whoever is listening that we are fated to be together. I'm thankful I was drawn into his world.

I make my own destiny, but sometimes, it's okay to be happy with someone that falls into your life. Or the other way around, in this instance. Sometimes, Fate knows what it's doing.

And that person that enters your orbit? Well, they might just be the love of your life, after all. Even if they're a tiny bit mad.

Chapter 21

We step back through the portal to find the room exactly how we left it, minus the tea party guests who traveled through the portal with us in the first place. White is still sitting in the same spot, constantly checking his watch. What he sees in that watch face, I have no idea. I plan on asking him that soon. Cheshire has his feet up on the table again, a toothpick sticking from the corner of his lips. He looks incredibly bored as he flicks open a pocket knife over and over again. Tweedledee and Tweedledum sit further down the table, as motionless as statues. Dum blinks, and I'm reminded that they are, in fact, alive and not just wax figures of the twins. No one is talking or paying attention to each other.

White looks up as we walk further into the room. When his eyes land on the Queen, he jumps from his seat, quicker than my eyes can follow. He sprints across the ballroom towards us. Cheshire looks at him quizzically before he notices the Queen. He stands, too, pocketing the knife before he walks across the room in our direction at a much slower swagger than White. The twins show no emotion whatsoever. They just watch blankly. Doesn't seem like they care about the old Queen then.

"White! Cheshire!" the Queen exclaims, opening her arms wide.

White walks right into her embrace, but instead of being able to hug her, he walks right through her. It startles me so badly that I squeak before I remember what Hatter had said. She's essentially a ghost. No one will be able to touch her.

White looks stricken for a moment before he gathers himself, straightens his waistcoat, and smiles.

"You look lovely as ever, your majesty."

"Yes," she giggles. "Death does wonders for your appearance."

White frowns, but he doesn't comment. Cheshire stands a healthy distance away, watching.

"Cheshire." She smiles at him. She doesn't try a hug again as she looks at him fondly. "How I've missed you all." She glances towards the Tweedles. "Even you two."

The twins nod their head cordially but don't respond. The queen dismisses them, not giving them any more of her attention.

"Come," the Hatter says. "Let us sit down for tea. You'll be able to enjoy the options, your majesty. The table is enchanted to enable the deceased a meal."

"It's been so long since I've sat down to the Mad Hatter's Tea Party."

She flutters her eyelashes at the Hatter when he offers her his arm. She seems to be able to hover her ghostly hand over his, giving the appearance that they're actually walking arm and arm. I watch them walk away, chatting animatedly about nonsense. My skin is still crawling from having been in the Hereafter and almost fading for the second time. It's almost like my body needs time to get used to its own skin again. It's an odd feeling, to almost die, knowing how close you are. I trust the Hatter, trust him to make sure I always come back, but that doesn't make the feelings disappear. I have skirted death too many times since I fell down the Rabbit Hole and yet, I don't seem to be worried. My priorities have obviously changed since I've been here. I just hope I have them in order.

White follows behind the Hatter and the Queen, taking his seat at the table with them. Cheshire still stands beside me, his eyes looking towards the portal gate longingly.

I worry my bottom lip between my teeth, shifting uncomfortably.

"She said to tell you she loves you. And to stay out of trouble," I whisper, sure he'll hear me.

Cheshire's eyes jerk to mine, some emotion flaring, strong enough to make my heart hurt. I fight the pain there, knowing Cheshire won't accept my empathy.

"She spoke to you." It isn't a question, but I answer anyways.

"Yes. She's amazing. And Beautiful." I mean it. I can see Danica and I becoming fast friends in the Hereafter. I just wish it was a possibility in the land of the living.

"Was," Cheshire bites. "She *was* amazing. She *was* beautiful. Now, she's just dead."

I'm shocked at the anger radiating from Cheshire, the rage simmering in his eyes as they meet mine. There's so much there, so much repressed. His eyes go full cat, turning into a thin slit and glowing bright-yellow. His ears lay flat on his head.

"Cheshire, I didn't mean— "

"Back off, Clara. Go back to your Hatter."

"But she's there, and she seems happy. She might not be in this world, but she exists. When it's your time, you'll see her again."

Cheshire looks at me, really studies my face.

"Didn't Hatter tell you a Son of Wonderland can't die?"

Realization dawns on me. I open my mouth, unsure of what is going to come out. Nothing does. Instead, I end up closing it again, my eyes watering from the pain I see reflected in his eyes. What do you say to someone when they know the worst pain? When they know they'll never again see someone they love? There's nothing I can say to make that better. Nothing.

"Spare me the water works, Clara. I don't need the pity." He looks towards the table where the Queen is laughing, White and Hatter smiling along with her. "Save it for someone who deserves it."

He starts walking towards the doors, obviously intending to leave the awkward and sad situation I had walked right into. I don't try to stop him this time. What else can I say? 'I'm so sorry you won't ever see your sister again' doesn't seem like it will cut it. I'm beginning to see that Wonderland isn't the only thing damaged. Its inhabitants are suffering just as much if not more. The Hatter's mind is like a prison, driving him mad. White's incessant watch checking has to be from something, some form of obsession birthed from horror. And

Cheshire. Cheshire is angry. Angry at the Red Queen, angry at me, angry at the world. That anger is going to eat him alive.

Cheshire is halfway to the doors when they slam open, the wood panels making marks in the walls on either side where they crash into the plaster. The Knave stands framed, Dormouse held up in front of him, bloody and broken. I watch in horror as the Knave tosses his body onto the ballroom floor at his feet. Bright red begins to pool beneath him, and I gasp. Dormouse isn't breathing. Dormouse isn't going to tell Cheshire to keep his boots off the table ever again. I take a step forward, no idea what I mean to do.

The Queen makes a strangled sound, her hand covering her mouth at the scene in front of us. The Knave glances at her but doesn't acknowledge her identity. It doesn't even seem like there's recognition there. I begin to worry our plan might not work.

"Sorry I'm late for tea," the Knave announces. "But I come bearing gifts."

He opens his arms wide, and Cards begin spilling into the room.

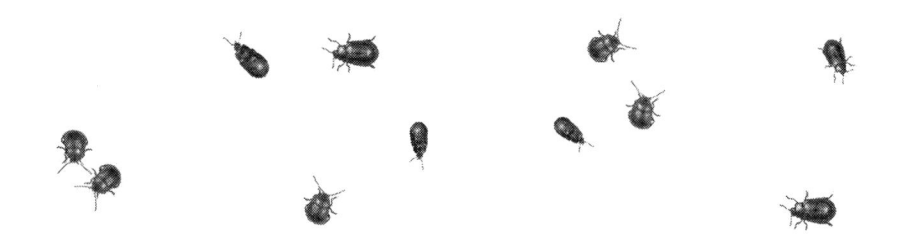

Chapter 22

I'm too far away from the Hatter. He's across the ballroom, and I'm too far away. It's the first thought that goes through my head when he spins and sprints towards me. Everything moves in slow motion, the sounds going away until it feels like I'm in a tunnel, like my ears are stuffed with cotton. The Queen stands from her seat, horror written across her face as she stares at her son's appearance, at the roses. I have a fleeting thought that I should have warned her. Tweedledum and Tweedledee hardly react. They certainly don't stand from their seats. The only reason I assume they know something is happening is because I see them both smile at the same time, their focus on the Cards spilling into the room. It's safe to say they know the Cards are not friends.

Cheshire disappears from his spot faster than I've ever seen him, only to reappear beside White on the other end of the table. Both are holding wicked looking swords, both glowing a different color. I can't see any details, but I know they're intricate. White and Cheshire scream a battle cry and charge into the ambush, cutting down Cards at lightning speeds.

Hatter is fast, but he isn't fast enough. I watch in dismay as the Knave hurls a dagger through the air. It's aimed right at the Hatter, and panic seizes my heart.

"Watch out!" I scream, but my voice doesn't reach him in time. The dagger slams into the Hatter's shoulder, embedding itself deep.

He stumbles from the force, but he doesn't stop. Blood rushes from the wound, dripping down his bare chest in tiny rivers.

He grabs my hand and drags me towards the portal gateway, ripping his hat from his head. Escape. We're trying to escape.

"We must go. We must go," he chants as he flings the hat at the ground.

Nothing happens.

Hatter makes a strangled noise and tries again, picking up the hat and throwing it down, putting all of his focus into the task. His face scrunches up as he tries to draw on his power. The sound of the Knave's laughter reaches our ears.

"Did you think I wouldn't plan for that this time?" The Knave asks, walking towards us, taking slow measured steps.

The Queen trails behind him. He hardly reacts to her, choosing to ignore his mother in favor of harming us.

"Alexander," she tries. Nothing. "Please, you must stop this."

The Knave takes his time walking towards us, like he doesn't have a care in the world. Behind him, the Cards are still spilling into the room, their numbers growing. White and Cheshire meet them, swinging their swords and snarling, bodies piling up around them at an alarming rate. It doesn't seem to be affecting the sheer number of enemies. Tweedledum is raking his claws down the chest of one. I look away just as Tweedledee grabs one of the Cards and rips his head clean from his body. My stomach rolls. Now I know why I feel like prey around them.

"The knife." The Hatter yanks the metal from his shoulder, its serrated edge ripping free. He screams in pain, blood spurting from the wound before he drops the blade to the floor. It clatters, sending droplets of bright red blood across the worn, golden floor. Some of it splatters my boots.

"It's enchanted." The knave smiles. "Made especially for the Hatter by the Red Queen. You should consider yourself special since she spent so much time on you."

"Alice can go to Hell," Hatter snarls.

I stand there while they spit words back and forth, unsure of what

I should be doing. I have the Heart Breaker in my hand, hoping I don't have to use it. My job is to stop this, to bring down the Knave. I don't want to hurt him, but we're at his mercy. I refuse to let more Wonderland inhabitants die. I need to step up now, before it's too late. My eyes search for the Queen, finding her right behind Alexander. Her face is sad, but she's strong. Her spine is stiff. I give her the barest nod, letting her know it's her time to act, to save her son. She walks forward.

She's beside the Knave when he swings a sword I never see him draw. It's aimed right for her neck, but it passes right through the same way White had. When it doesn't harm her, the Knave's eyes widen slightly, and I see the first signs of recognition in their depths. The Queen, to her credit, doesn't slow or show any reaction that she notices the sword pass through her. She's continues walking until she stands beside us.

"Alexander." She focuses her eyes on the man she birthed, taking in everything he has become. "My baby. How I've missed you."

"I belong to no one but the Red Queen!" he snarls, taking a step towards us threateningly.

Hatter and I draw the swords we wear at the same time, the sounds they make as they slide from the sheaths drawing the Knave's eyes. I had already slipped the Heart Breaker away, deciding we are too close for the bullets to safely hit only the Knave. There are too many on our team in the line of fire.

"You think to best me in battle?" he asks. The question is directed at me. I raise my chin.

"It's my destiny," I reply, holding the sword steady at my side.

He laughs, and I tense.

"That caterpillar has been filling your heads with nonsense, has he? You actually think any of that is true?"

I smile at him, and I know it's not a friendly smile. I can feel the menace I have yet to let show, dripping from my lips. My rage overtakes me, but when I speak again, my voice is calm, steady. The Hatter stiffens beside me, my darkness licking against him.

"We don't know if it's true. But we hope it is. We have hope for Wonderland. And I'm going to brandish that Hope like a sword."

"Your hope will die with you." The Knave lifts his sword.

"Alexander. This isn't you," the Queen tries again. "This is not the boy I raised. My son would never raise his sword to friends."

"I'm not a boy. I'm a man. In the highest station possible."

"No, my son. You were a prince. Now, you're nothing but a puppet."

"Shut up!" the Knave snarls. "You don't know what you're talking about!"

"I know my son. And I love him. I know he's somewhere inside you, fighting to get out. Let him out." The Queen takes a step closer, her eyes glistening as she tries to reason with the Knave. I hope against all hope that Alexander is still in there, still able to find his way home. "This is not who you are."

"You know nothing! You will all die for the lies spilling from your lips. I will remove your heads and take them to the Queen on a silver platter." The Knave looks at the Hatter. "Can you survive a beheading, Hatter? Shall we test it?" Blinding rage fills my body, but I hold myself in check. I breathe in and out the same way I do in the courtroom. I need to keep a level head. Wars are not won with rash decisions. They're won with strategy.

"I cannot die." Hatter's voice is rough, and I have no doubt that the memories that come flooding back are nothing less than gruesome.

"Well, then I suppose the Red Queen will keep your head in a glass box where you'll be forced to watch everyone you love, your entire world, die at the hands of the One True Queen. She'll bathe in their blood, and she won't stop until every last corpse is cold at her feet. I'll watch you scream out in your glass box until you shred your vocal cords to ribbons."

Hatter jerks, the blow hitting him deep. I try to grab his hand, feeling the tension coil up, ready to explode. I'm too slow. I'm always too slow. He charges the Knave, his sword raised high. There's a clash of metal as their blades meet, the clanging mixing with those of the fight around us.

White, Cheshire, and the Tweedles are fighting hard, but the Cards outnumber them ten to one. The more they kill, the more that pour in, like a hydra. Cut off one head, and two more take its place. I watch the Tweedles leave a trail of carnage behind them, but even then it doesn't seem to be enough. Tweedledum is bleeding from a huge gash on his chest, the dragon-scale armor ripped open. Tweedledee has blood dripping down her horns. Bloody, they make a gruesome sight.

White is completely covered in the gore of battle. He's dripping blood, the spray soaking his clothes. I can't tell if any of it is his or if it's all from the Cards he has fallen. His ears twitch, cataloging movements around him. He seems to know seconds before a Card charges him, able to dance out of the way. Cheshire is completely spotless everywhere besides the scary looking claws on his hands. They drip the blood of the Cards he mutilates, leaving puddles everywhere as he makes his way through the group. He rips them apart one by one, his body full feline. They're both a sight to behold.

When I focus back on the Hatter and the Knave, I can tell they are equally matched. They dance back and forth, swinging their swords. Hatter seems stronger, but he's injured, and I'm beginning to think his mind is playing tricks on him. Every now and then he adds an extra swing in a different direction, like he thinks someone is there rushing towards him. There's never anyone there, and the Knave takes every opportunity to take advantage of his open ribs. Hatter is bleeding from cuts running up the side of his body. Every clang of metal makes my heart squeeze that much harder.

"We have to do something." I state the obvious, looking at the Queen for inspiration.

"What can we do? He won't listen to me."

"We need something powerful," I mumble, watching the fight closely. "Something that will work."

"Like what?" the Queen's voice shakes. She wrings her hands together.

"Is there anything you can say? Anything that will make him remember the time before he became the Knave? Something that will trigger a strong emotion? Anything at all." It's my final plea before I have to call the plan a failure and return to the idea that I have to kill a man more victim than a villain. If I can avoid that, I will, but the odds don't look good.

"I, yes. There might be. There's a lullaby."

"What lullaby? He'll recognize it?"

She smiles slightly, even though Chaos surrounds us. "When Alexander was a baby, I used to sing a lullaby for him every night. When he got too old for such things, I still hummed it around the castle. He never liked to admit it, but I caught him listening to the sound a lot, enraptured the same way he'd been as a young child. I wrote the song for him, when he was born."

"We have to try it then. It's our last chance." I turn, meeting her eyes, making sure she hears me. "This is it. If we fail, we find another way to get rid of the Knave. We won't have any other choice."

She nods even though I just told her I might have to kill her son. There's too much at stake, and the Knave is the Red Queen's greatest weapon. If we fail, Wonderland dies. She understands even as her heart breaks. There won't be any other way.

The Queen stands tall, folding her hands in front of her. Her eyes begin to water even before she opens her mouth, the tears spilling over her lashes and onto her cheeks. When she begins to sing, I feel the pain she's infusing into the words, the agony of a lost child. Tears spring to my own eyes, and I dash them away as they fall.

"Hush now, my baby.
Be still, love, don't cry.
It's time to rest your golden head.
Dragons will chase you
My sweet little knight,
When you lay down in your bed.
Vanquish the evil,

Help up the weak,
Wear your humble crown with pride.
My strong little boy,
Stay true to yourself,
There is no reason to hide.
Hush now, my baby,
Rest your golden head,
And turn your face towards the sun.
All of those shadows
Will fall behind, my star,
Your journey has barely begun."

When the Queen had first begun the song, the ballroom was filled with the sounds of battle, her voice drowned out by the clanging metal and the screams of anger. When she finishes, the ballroom is eerily silent, the last notes of the lullaby floating through the air.

Tears flow freely down my face as I watch. The Knave stills mid-swing, turning to stare at his mother. Hatter watches him warily, holding his arm where blood runs from a gash. None of us dare move.

"Mother," the Knave rasps.

The eye I can see is black, the blue hidden by the intense power of the Queen, the darkness swallowing up the pupil and everything else inside. I watch in wonder as the black fades away, revealing a blue so clear, it looks like the water in travel brochures. I take a startled step back. The Knave's eye moves to me, and comprehension crosses his face. There's awe in there, surprise, hope. The hope makes my face scrunch in an attempt to hold back the water works.

"You've done it. You found the loophole."

I watch in shock as the roses on his face and chest whither and die, and for a moment, I feel victory dancing at my heels. My chest feels a little bit lighter.

"I want to save you," I choke out. "I don't want to kill you."

"I don't need saving," he snarls, blackness dancing at the edge of his eye.

"Sweetheart," the Queen jumps in, drawing his attention back to her. The blackness disappears again. "This isn't you."

"I'm the Red Queen's slave." The words are pained, anger and sadness mixed together. "Alice betrayed me."

"Alice betrayed us all. You are not the Red Queen's slave. You do not belong to Alice." The Queen raises her chin. "You are Prince Alexander, the rightful King of Wonderland. You will fight this hold she has on you. You will fight for us all."

"That part of me is dead. I'm not that man anymore."

"He's in there somewhere, fighting to get out. You are stronger than this. You are a King."

Tears leak from his eye, his body tensing.

"I'm not strong enough to keep her out. Even now, I can feel her power moving through me, seeking to take root again."

I believe him. A bright red rose blooms on his forehead, only one. I feel the scale we're standing on, this balancing act as we fight to see who can gather the most weight. For a moment, I believed we had tipped the scales in our favor. I had believed we could do this without bloodshed. When I see another red rose bloom, my eyes seek out the Hatter's. He notices the roses, too. His face is anguished, and I realize this isn't something he wants to do either. We had both placed all our hope on this plan. We had both fought hard to save a life that isn't meant to be taken. It's too soon. Alexander needs to live. We're so close but not close enough. We're losing the battle.

"You can fight this," the Queen urges. "I love you, Alexander. Your father and I love you very much."

"Stop it," the Knave whispers.

"We love you, Alexander. You are stronger than she is. You will fight this!" There's panic in the Queen's voice now as another rose blooms, this time on his chest. "You will fight her!"

"Stop talking."

"We wish we could have protected you all those years ago. We wish we could have spared you this agony. We're always with you."

"Stop it!" The Knave is screaming now, his hands coming up to grasp handfuls of his hair. He tugs brutally at the roots. The veins on his neck begin to bulge at the strain of fighting off the Red Queen's influence. I cringe, clenching my fists tight. My chest hurts, my heart beating frantically inside.

There's a blinding light in the room, one that causes my eyes to close. I can't see past the stars in my vision, can't breathe for fear something worse has come. When I peek past my lashes again, Danica stands beside me in all her glory, her tail curling around my ankles, her form of comfort. She's wearing the same golden dress, the same serene smile. A strangled noise comes from somewhere in the room, like someone can't breathe. I don't look, but I know it's Cheshire, know the noises are choked off sobs. I fight the surprise from my face, giving nothing away as I steel myself for whatever this means.

"Danica," the Knave whispers. A rose shrivels on his face.

"Hello, Alexander." Her voice is soft, threads of love woven through the words. I meet the Hatter's shocked eyes, my own reflecting the same emotion. Danica. He loves Danica, too.

Agony is written across the Knave's face, his hands gripping his forehead tight.

"I can't hold her back," he cries, his face red from the effort. "I can't stop her."

"Fight it," Danica says. "You're stronger than she is."

"Not anymore." The Knave falls to his knees, his sword clattering to the marble. "Not anymore."

Danica moves closer, falling to her knees before him. Her hands reach up and brush his skin. There's a bright light where they touch even though Danica isn't corporeal. Another rose falls away, but it's replaced by two more. He looks up at Danica, tears trailing down his cheek.

"I'm sorry," he wheezes. "I'm so sorry."

"We will not discuss that. Not now. You will fight her. Fight her. For me. For Wonderland."

"She's coming back. I feel it taking hold again. I can't win." The

Knave's eye looks towards me, and clarity shines from within. "The prophecy," he whispers. I shake my head. "Yes! You must! Kill me now! While you still have the chance. I can't stop her. I can't win."

"You can't help what you've done. You're a victim. You deserve to live."

Everything in my nature rebels against punishing an innocent man. My soul bleeds for what he's asking me to do, and my fear of having to do it is shattering. I want to help people. I want to help them all. Do no harm. Do no harm. Do no harm.

"You have to kill me," he roars, his face blooming with more roses. The wound on his face is almost completely covered again. He's losing the battle. "I can't hold her off much longer."

The Queen cries in dismay, realizing that this is it. This is the moment we feared. She rushes forward to wrap her arms around his shoulders, the same bright light emanating from her as Danica. There's a ringing in my ears as time slows down, and I clutch my heart in dismay. A phantom wind spins through the room, creating a vortex that lifts loose strands of my hair around my face. My eyes leak a trail of never-ending tears.

At some point, the Hatter moves, coming to stand beside me. He holds my hand in his, his face written with the same agony as mine. There's a sword in his other hand, a sword he holds out to me.

"Stab me through the chest," the Knave begs. He opens his arms wide, Danica and the Queen clinging to his shoulders.

"I can't," I choke. "I can't do this."

"You must! This is your duty! You must save Wonderland! You must save us all!" His voice chokes on the words, desperation taking hold.

The Hatter moves, wrapping his arms around me from behind. His palms fold mine over the pommel of the sword, holding them together as if he's afraid I'll let go. He doesn't move them, and we end up holding the sword aloft together. I shake my head, no longer able to speak.

"You must!"

The Queen is crying, her arms wrapped around her son tightly.

She's nothing more than smoke, but her arms seem to steady the Knave, giving him strength. Danica has tears running down her cheeks as well, her hands now gripping either side of his face, keeping his eyes on hers. They stare at each other, memorizing. If we do this, we'll be spearing the sword through her first. My arms begin to shake.

"It's okay," Alexander whispers to them. "It's okay."

Danica leans forward and places her lips against his. It's the barest of touches, and where they touch, they glow a pretty green. The wind picks up, and I hear things begin to crash off the table, the gusts tearing through everything. When she pulls away, his eye finds me again.

"Please," he sobs. "I don't want to be this monster anymore."

I can barely see, the tears spilling from my eyes, blurring my vision. But the Hatter helps me take a step forward, and then another, until we're in front of Alexander, and Danica, and the Queen.

"Together," Hatter whispers in my ear. "You are not alone, Clara."

I don't fight as we lift our arms. I understand what has to be done. Black dances at the edge of Alexander's eye, seeking to take over. Roses are blooming rapidly across his chest. He's losing the battle, and he's willing to forfeit his life in order to save the world he should have ruled. His sacrifice will save us all.

"May you fly on the wings of Wonder, your Majesty." The words come automatically to my lips. I have no knowledge of it being appropriate or tradition, but it seems to be the right thing to say. "May you embrace the freedom of death."

His spine straightens as he looks me in the eyes. He nods, his jaw clenching hard against the pain he has to be in. Tendons throb in his neck, veins ready to burst in his forehead, as he strains against the Red Queen.

"Do it now!" he screams, every word agony. "Do it now!"

Together, Hatter and I tighten our grip. We step forward, thrusting the gleaming sword deep, right in the center of the blooming roses on his chest. The air stills, the room grows quiet. I watch as blood wells around the sword, running down his chest in small rivers before pooling on the floor beneath his knees. The black drains away. The roses wither once more and fall to the ground as ash. The Queen quietly sobs. Danica keeps her hands on Alexander's face, holding onto him, letting him know he isn't alone.

Another blinding light fills the room, so powerful, I can feel its warmth. I close my eyes, but when I open them again, spots dance across my vision. When I'm finally able to blink them away, Alexander kneels before us in golden glory, the sword still protruding from his chest. Here's the man from my visions, the one who was meant to be King.

Danica clutches onto him, her hands holding his face still as blood drips from the corner of his mouth. She doesn't move, doesn't waver. The Queen clutches his hand to her as the Prince fixes two clear blue eyes on me. A bronze crown sits across his brow, golden hair spilling over his forehead. He smiles just the tiniest bit.

"Thank you." The words are free of pain. They're clear, but they're soft. I have a moment where I think, this is it. We can still save him. He's free from her clutches. But then, he collapses to the ground, into the pooled blood beneath him. He doesn't move again.

I turn in the Hatter's arms and bury my face in his chest, uncaring of the blood still there, letting my tears flow free. I cry for the brutality of the World the Red Queen has made. I cry for the mother and woman who lost a son and a lover, not once but twice. But mostly, I cry for the sacrifice one man made to save his Wonderland.

I cry until there are no more tears to give.

Chapter 23

I shouldn't be surprised when I come downstairs a few hours later to find everything back to a creepy sense of normal. The entryway is immaculate even though when I had walked through on my way to the room, it had been covered in blood and most of the furniture destroyed. Dormouse had taken a few Cards with him. He hadn't gone down without a fight. Now, as I pass through on my way to the ballroom, everything is in its proper place, not a single thing is left broken. There's the mended vase, the designs curling smoke and grotesque dragons. It sits unbroken on top of a table, black and purple flowers arranged inside. The tiles that had been smashed or cracked are once again smooth, no evidence left that they had ever been damaged. The entry is silent. No one bangs at the door. No echoes reach my ears. The only sounds are that of my breath and the shuffle of my clothing.

There is no Dormouse.

When I step from the last stair, his presence is sorely missed, even if he never spared me more than, "He's in the ballroom."

I had debated about coming back down from my room at all. This tea party would be fuller than ever, and I doubt my heart can stand to look at those I failed. But I owe them this. If they could sacrifice their lives for the greater cause, then I could sit down at a table with them and meet their eyes. I can remind them there's still hope for Wonderland.

I open the giant ballroom doors myself, the ominous creak they always make alerting everyone inside that I'm coming in. Hatter glances up at me, a warm smile on his face even though his eyes are sad. I can't bring myself to return it yet, the emotions floating beneath the surface of my skin holding precedence. Everything hurts, my body, my soul, my heart. Faced with the people who took part in that suffering, who are the reason I hurt, I can't bring myself to show happiness.

Hatter isn't alone at the table, of course. Today, it's almost completely full. The sheer amount of people filling the table shocks me. I didn't realize that the Queen's cards would be guests, assuming they are little more than faceless minions. As I look out at all the unfamiliar faces, I can't believe that each one is a person who had been trapped much the same way as Prince Alexander. That means there's even more people I failed to save.

Prince Alexander sits down at the end of the table, close to the Hatter. His mother sits on one side of him. Danica sits on the other. I had hoped Cheshire would sit next to Danica, a chance for them to visit, but Danica only seems to have eyes for the Prince, and Cheshire only has eyes for the tea cup in front of him. Both Cheshire and White sit on the other side of the table, across from them. Cheshire looks like he's trying to set the table on fire with his intense gaze, his tail flicking from side to side behind him. Even his ears are laid flat on his head. Why isn't anyone acknowledging the tension there? White looks tense, checking his watch as usual. He's sitting at the end of the table, the very first chair where I typically sit.

The Tweedles sit in the midst of the Cards, sipping their tea delicately. They don't eye the guests around them anymore. They seem content to just belong, full with whatever it is they needed to feed on. It's an odd thing to watch them sit so regally when a few hours ago, I watched them tear through the Cards with their bare hands.

Dormouse sits right beside the Hatter, opposite White and beside Danica. There's a small smile on his face as he watches me stand in the doorway, my brain a mess of emotions. As I take a step into the room, someone begins to clap. The sound builds until everyone is clapping, all besides Cheshire, White, and The Hatter. Hatter understands I don't want to be celebrated for failing, for having to kill the man I was attempting to save. I know there had been no other choice and that we had tried our best. I will eventually make peace with that, but for now, I want nothing more than to forget the sound a blade makes as it slides past skin and bone.

I'm not sure why Cheshire and White don't join in the clapping. Perhaps they realize what it took for me to be able to perform the duty, that I had to lose a piece of myself in the process. Perhaps they realize that Wonderland has started to feed on me, warp me, starting to change my soul the same way it has done theirs. Perhaps they understand exactly what I'm going through.

I make my way across the room, towards the empty seat that is left just for me. It's no longer off to the side of the table, no longer in my usual spot. We now have chairs equally side by side at the head, where we'll both preside over tea parties together from now on. It's my way of giving back to those we lose, to help them have one last meal. It's my way of supporting the Hatter and helping him to stay strong. I won't stop helping those still living, but I'm also going to help the dead. I'm going to keep fighting for Wonderland's freedom. I won't stop fighting the Red Queen. Not until it's my turn to cross into the Hereafter. And even then, I'll have my Hatter beside me.

I take my seat in the golden ornate chair that matches the Hatter's black one. It still has the skulls, the details, but it seems brighter somehow. The cushion is still the Hatter's signature purple. I feel small as I sit on the velvet seat, like I'm a child playing dress up, like I have no idea what I'm actually doing. But this is my world now, and I will be the beacon that they need. It doesn't stop me from feeling as lost as little Alice, or as mad as the Hatter. Perhaps that's why I chose to wear the outfit I'm in. Perhaps, I needed to feel more like myself right now, to ground myself.

"I like what you're wearing," the Hatter leans over and whispers in my ear. The table resumes its chatter, giving us the tiniest bit of privacy.

"Really?" I take a sip of the tea in front of me. A chocolate rose flavor coats my tongue, and I savor the taste. It mimics the flavors of the Reali-Tea closely but without the added metallic taste. This one is the Hatter's special Blend, the healing kind. Does he think he can heal my soul?

"I think you look radiant."

I look at the Hatter, raising an eyebrow. I'm wearing skinny jeans and a t-shirt I blessedly found in the back of my wardrobe. The jeans are black, like most things are here, but the shirt is bright, eye-catching pink. I can't find any shoes besides the combat boots and heels, so I chose the boots. Not quite myself but close enough. My hair is piled on top of my head, a few wet strands falling around my face and curling at the nape of my neck.

"You are the most beautiful thing I have ever seen," Hatter reiterates. "Beautiful enough to be my queen."

I frown at him, my dislike for the word strong.

"I'm not a queen."

"No," he smiles. "You're right. You're my Clara Bee. My Hattress."

There's such joy on his face that I'm hopeless. I return the smile with a small one, taking his hand in mine.

Laughter fills the room as the table bustles with lively chatter. The clatter of plates and dishes adds to the fray when food appears on the table, turning almost overwhelming to my ears. I nibble at a meat pie in front of me. It's warm and much better than the sweets I've been eating. I don't ask what the meat is. Some things are just best left unknown.

I watch the table, my shoulders relaxing at the celebration of it. I keep finding my eyes drifting over to the Knave, to Prince Alexander. I fulfilled my part of the prophecy. I downed the Knave. He doesn't look sad, or angry. In fact, he looks more peaceful than I've ever seen him, his face full of joy as his mother dotes on him, and Danica meets his eyes. It eases the pain just a tiny bit, knowing he's happy, knowing he's free if not alive.

Hatter raises his teacup into the air in front of him, and the room falls silent, their eyes riveted to us.

"To the first of the Triad." His voice carries down the table, reaching everyone's ears easily. "To my Clara Bee."

I blush under the attention, but I don't look away as everyone lifts their own teacups into the air. Even the Tweedles lift theirs.

"To Wonderland and Prince Alexander," I add before we all take a sip together. The Prince meets my eyes, a small smile on his face. I nod to him, and he returns the gesture. It seems we are both at an understanding. We have both sacrificed something.

There's this sense of belonging as we all place the teacups back on their saucers. There's this feeling like I'm exactly where I'm supposed to be, like I'm home. I find myself smiling just a little bit wider at the thought. I'm home.

Later, after everyone has stuffed their faces with cakes and sweets and gorged themselves on tea, I venture the question that has been begging to be asked.

"So, what now?" I'm only the first of three. We've won a battle, but we haven't won the war.

"We find the second of the triad," Hatter answers, a happy gleam in his eyes. "Well, White does." Hatter hasn't been able to keep the love from sparkling in their depths all night. Cheshire has already called him out on it once, calling it disgusting that we keep making googly eyes at each other, but Hatter waves the words away. His hands stay touching me, whether it's his hand on my knee or our fingers laced together. It's like we're both afraid of what'll happen if we let go. My eyes flick to the bandage on his shoulder, the stiffness that he holds it with. A son of Wonderland can't die, but he can feel pain. Healing isn't instantaneous. He heals faster than I would, but it's still slow.

I look over at White who is checking his watch for the thousandth time.

"That's your mate up next."

White looks up at me and nods, his lips curling up at the corners.

"If she's able to accept Wonderland and all that. I imagine it's a bit disorienting to fall down a Rabbit Portal."

"It is indeed," I agree, remembering my own fall. I was certain I had been kidnapped and drugged at first. My eyes trail over to Cheshire after taking a sip of my tea. "And then you're the third."

Cheshire scoffs, rolling his eyes at the words.

"No, thanks."

"But it's prophesy," White exclaims, looking aghast.

"And it's also bullshit. We got lucky the first time. Clara did exactly what the prophecy says she would. That doesn't mean the next two will. And it doesn't mean they won't be useless twits."

"Cheshire," Danica scolds. "There's no reason to tempt Fate with this dismissal. If you keep pushing, Fate will decide you need to be taught a lesson."

"At least, it'll be a better lesson than I've learned from you."

Danica stiffens, her eyes widening just slightly. I take Hatter's hand, waiting for the explosion.

"And what's that supposed to mean?" she asks, her voice shaky.

"You're holding hands with your murderer who—surprise!—was also your lover." Cheshire's lips curl back in a snarl. "You're dead because you couldn't accept the Red Queen could take over your royal boy toy. I always thought you didn't move that day for fear, that you were frozen with terror as the Knave bore down on you. I didn't know it was because you loved him and thought that would be enough."

"That's enough," Hatter interrupts. "I will not have this at my table."

Danica's eyes are glistening with unshed tears. She fights to hold them back, but one still trickles over the edge, trailing slowly down her cheek. Cheshire tracks its course, his face softening slightly. He looks down at the table, staring at his plate. Shame colors his face red.

"I'm sorry, Danica," he mumbles. "I just, I miss you." Everyone hears the words. Everyone feels the pain as Cheshire fades away, disappearing under the penetrating eyes of the table. His last words float through the air, reaching our ears. "I, alone, decide my fate."

There's crushing silence for a moment before someone speaks.

"I'm sorry," Danica sniffs. "I didn't mean for that to come up."

I wave her apology away.

"Don't worry about it. It's none of our business. Besides, emotions are high right now."

White glances at his watch again and stands up.

"You're leaving already?" I ask, a small smile curling my lips.

"I'd best go find the second." He turns to walk away but looks over his shoulder at me. "Wish me luck."

"You don't need it, White. Just be you." I wonder what woman is a match for the White Rabbit.

"Oh, I don't know about that," he smirks. Then he disappears from the room. I hear the front door close behind him.

"There's a lot more to White than I realize, huh?" I look at Hatter who is already looking at me. Love shines from his eyes. He leans forward and kisses my lips softly, briefly, before leaning away.

"We sons of Wonderland are a handful. We're all damaged in some way. White may not seem it, but he's just as broken as both Cheshire and I."

"You're not broken, Hatter," I whisper, kissing the back of his hand. "Not anymore."

The tea party goes on long into the night, everyone too wrapped up in the feeling of hope to worry about the hour. Hatter finally has to stand and announce that it's time to go. We all stand together. This occasion, I'm not accompanying Hatter into the Hereafter. He doesn't want the stress of fading a third time to start to wear on me. Twice is already enough. So, I say my goodbyes to everyone at the gateway. The Queen gives me a tight hug, a hug I'm surprised I'm able to feel before she steps through the portal. Something about the enchantments of the room Hatter supplies. It allows everyone a last goodbye. Danica is next, embracing me like a friend. I keep looking for Cheshire, hoping he'll show back up and tell his sister goodbye. I'm disappointed when he doesn't.

"Take care of Cheshire for me," she whispers, tears in her eyes. I chuckle, the sound watery at my own unshed tears.

"I'll try my best, but I can't promise he'll let me."

"He's a big softie really."

I don't have the heart to tell her that Cheshire probably isn't the same as he was last time she saw him. Wonderland is wearing on him, breaking him down. Losing his sister was probably difficult. Losing himself is probably agonizing. When she passes through the portal with a last smile at the Prince, the Cards begin filing in after her. They each wave to me as they pass, saying their thank yous. I don't deserve a thank you, but I return their smiles with a nod of my head. Prince Alexander stands next to me, watching the progress. There are a lot of them.

"It's not your fault," he breaks the silence. "You did what you had to do."

"That doesn't make it any easier to live with."

"No." He shakes his head. "No, it doesn't." He smiles sadly at me. "Wonderland is dying, Clara. I may not be alive anymore, but the rest of Wonderland still is. Save it for me."

He kisses me on the cheek before stepping towards the portal.

"Alexander," I call. He stops and looks back at me, the portal colors illuminating him from behind, giving him a celestial appearance. "I'm sorry I couldn't save you."

He smiles again, this time the happiness pours from him.

"But you did, Clara. And you'll save us all."

Then he steps through the portal. The colors disappear, and I'm left alone in the Hatter's ballroom.

Chapter 24

The trek to my room is quiet and eerie. I have no idea where the Tweedles are, and I don't know if I want to know where they sleep or if they even need to. If they sleep in the basement like vampires, it's none of my business.

The house creaks and groans as I make my way through the hallways. I push open my purple door and step inside. The room is lit by the fireplace, warming the chill air. I immediately head to the bathroom, turning the faucets until steaming hot water begins flowing out. I pour in some of the bottles that smell like lavender, the fragrance relaxing my body as the scent reaches my nose.

I stare at the bubbles beginning to form, lost in thought before I finally begin stripping out of my clothes. I had cleaned up after the events of the ballroom, washing away the blood and the grime, but I just want to relax now, to ease my mind. Too much has happened in such a short amount of time.

When I slip into the steaming water and relax my head against the rim of the claw foot tub, I begin to think of home, and what everyone thinks happened to me. In the vision, Hatter had said time works differently here. I've been gone a week in Wonderland time, but at home, it could have been months now. There would have been searches for me, suspects would have been questioned, the enemies I had made in the courtrooms. My employees, no doubt, spearheaded the campaign. They were the closest I had left of family but, even then, I hadn't felt like I belonged at their side. I just wanted to take care of them, to fight for the people that suffered the same fate as my father had. I had done pretty well. I hope my dad would have been proud.

Thankfully, I had a will drawn up when I had first started my law firm, stating what would happen in the event of my death or inability to retain my position. The company was to split its shares between every employee working for me at the time of death, or, in this case, disappearance. Pearl, my understudy, would receive full funding to complete her license so that she could take over my position. I wonder what they had all thought when my own lawyer had strolled in and told them they all now owned the company. I wonder what they thought of me taking care of them one last time. I hadn't told them about the will. I hadn't told anyone.

I have no desire to return to my world. Wonderland has revealed the broken pieces inside me even as it fixes them. I have always hungered for a family of my own since I lost my parents, for people who understand me and accept me as I am. I've found that here. Everything is a bit twisted, and chaotic, and downright scary sometimes, but I now think of it as my home. And I plan to fight for it and the ones I love.

Hatter steps around the corner, his eyes falling to my face where it sticks out of the mass of bubbles, some of them falling over the edge and onto the floor. The bubbles hide my body, but the way he looks at me, it's like he can see everything, all the way down to my soul.

He walks lazily into the room, shrugging out of his jacket and dropping it to the floor.

"Have you been relaxing?" he drawls, setting his hat on the vanity.

"A bit. Mostly I've been thinking."

"About what?"

"Home."

His hands pause where they had begun to unbutton his pants, and his eyes jerk up to mine. The gold there dulls just a little.

"Do you want to leave Wonderland?"

The way he asks it, equal parts fear and acceptance, sends arrows stabbing through my heart.

"I'm not going anywhere," I reply, my voice thick. "You're stuck with me."

He visibly relaxes, his shoulders loosening before he shoves his leather pants down, leaving him completely nude before me. I crook my finger at him when he hesitates, like he isn't sure if he should join me or not. He smiles, stepping forward and swinging his legs over. As he sinks slowly down into the bubbles, our legs intertwining, water spills over the sides, splashing against the marble floor. I chuckle softly, the feel of his skin slick against mine sending giddy waves through me. Hatter leans his head back, looking at me with heavy-lidded eyes.

"I don't think I could bear it if you left me," he whispers, and I frown. "If you left Wonderland."

"I couldn't bear it either, Hatter. I haven't even entertained the idea of leaving this terrifying world behind, of living without you."

He smiles at me softly, and it makes his face smooth out. His eyes glisten the barest amount, like he's so happy that tears threaten to fall. I know the feeling. I'm fighting them, as well, and losing. How can a prophecy know we fit so perfectly together? How can it know something so profound, that we can look past the madness, the chaos, and find love shining underneath?

I shift in the tub, more water splashing out as I wrap myself around the Hatter. My core bumps against his hardness, and we both suck in a breath at the contact. I kiss him softly on the lips before leaning my forehead against his, content to breathe him in and hold him to me.

"To think," I whisper. "I had to fall down a Rabbit Hole to find love." I sniffle, the emotions taking over. "I love you, Hatter."

His hands wrap around my waist, clutching me to him as if he's afraid I'll float away.

"Love is madness." He kisses the corner of my lips, my cheeks, the tip of my nose. "And I love you with all the Madness in my soul, Clara Bee."

Tears slip over my lashes, falling between us. He frantically begins wiping them away, and a husky laugh startles out of me. The

Hatter doesn't seem to be able to handle my tears. I slip down and place a lingering kiss on his chest, right over his heart beating steady and strong.

I look up into his eyes, a wide smile stretching my face.

"Then let's be mad together."

Mad as a Hatter

To be continued...

ACKNOWLEDGMENTS

First, I'd like to thank my son for being the reason I get up every day and write. Showing him that dreams can come true is alway forefront in my mind.

Thank you to my parents, for supporting me no matter what. I'm sure you wonder what goes on in my head sometimes but don't worry, I'm published now so it's legit. I love y'all so much.

Thank you to the family members that have been so supportive. Grandma, Grandpa, Martina, Kelly, Susie, Mark and the whole gang. I'm so happy y'all are behind me. I hope this one didn't freak y'all out too much. ::Runs away and hides::

Thank you so much to my Penned in Ink family. Without y'all, I wouldn't have gotten the kick in the butt I needed. The support is unreal and I'm glad to have made this journey with you all.

To my absolutely amazing CP's, Nicole JeRee, Elizabeth Clare, and Amara Kent. Words cannot express how much y'all have helped me. I'm glad we stumbled upon each other and formed the perfect group, even if we're all in different time zones around the world.

Thank you to Nicole JeRee again because she formatted this book and it's amazing. Thank you to Methyss Art for the amazing cover.

And finally, thank you to everyone reading this book. Thank you for taking a chance on a new author and I hope you stay along for the ride. Without you, this book would be nowhere.

If there's anyone I missed, I'm sorry. Know that I'm absolutely thankful for you all. I hope you enjoyed the Hatter and Clara's story. Welcome to my Wonderland.

Kendra Moreno was born and raised in Texas where, if the locusts don't drive you mad, the fire ants and sticker burrs will. Iced tea, or aptly called straight sugar, fuels her for battling the forces of evil and washing the never ending dishes her son dirties.

She has one husband who listens to her spin tall tales constantly without fail. Although he doesn't always know what she's talking about, he supports her like a high dollar brassier. Kendra has one son who will one day read her stories. For now she's teaching him that books are meant to be cherished and not destroyed. Her three Hellhounds keep her company while she writes.

If she isn't writing, you can usually find Kendra elbows deep in anything from paint to cookie dough.

> If you'd like to have a place to discuss the book with other fans, head over to Kendra's facebook group (Worlds of Wonder) where you can get updates on her work before anyone else.

amazon.com/author/kendramoreno
facebook.com/kendra.morenoauthor.7
instagram.com/writingbeast90

ALSO BY KENDRA MORENO

Sons of Wonderland:
Mad as a Hatter
Late as a Rabbit
Feral as a Cat

Anthologies:
Cupid's Playthings:
Supernova
At World's End: An Apocalypse Anthology:
Wings of Rage
Falling For Them Anthology Vol. 4:
Four Parts Super

Clockwork Butterfly
A Steampunk Reverse Harem

Printed in Germany
by Amazon Distribution
GmbH, Leipzig